First Lady

To A

Dope Boy

Written By

Bridgette I'esha

Published by Bridgette I'esha

Synopsis

Sharnese Jackson always wondered what it was like to experience love. Growing up with a mother who was scorned, all she ever received was pain. The abuse she endured at the hands of the woman who was supposed to love and protect her turned her heart cold. Every man that approached her, she turned down. She refused to let anyone inside her heart. That was until she met Murda. Green to the hood life, Sharnese has no idea how quickly her world is about to be turned upside down when she happens to fall in love with a dope boy.

Born into the world raised by a Pimp/ drug dealer for a father and former prostitute as a mother Cortez "Murda" Rodriguez is taught the dope game early in life. Being the biggest dope-boy in Brooklyn is no easy task when there are people determined to take him out.

Murda becomes infatuated with Sharnese from the very first day he lays eyes on her. Her looks, personality and the things she desired in life had him wanting to know more about the beauty. With an ongoing war in the streets, he knew Sharnese was the last thing he should've been focused on, but there was something about her that was different. While most women only found love in his money, she was interested in getting to know the real him. Not the savage and dope boy that everyone knew him as. Sharnese believes Murda is her knight in shining armor…. That's until his double life is revealed.

Left once again with a cold heart, Sharnese takes some time to get over Murda and ends up meeting Kas. Not wanting to jump into a new relationship. They start off as friends. Unaware that Kas is Murda's number one enemy in the streets.

Unbeknownst to both Murda and Kas, information is leaked that could either end their war or spark new flames. Can one secret end a street war or will it cause even more chaos? Will Sharnese be able to accept what happens when she becomes the First Lady to A Dope Boy?

Prologue

"Sharnese Jackson, get ya black ass in here right now!" Tonya screamed.

"Yes, Mom," Sharnese replied.

"Didn't I tell you I wanted my house cleaned spotless? That meant no dirty dishes in the sink at all," Tonya shook her head and looked at her daughter in pure disgust.

Sharnese glances over at the sink and sees a dirty cup and spoon that she knew wasn't in the sink before. She had spent the entire day in the house cleaning. Fear overcame her body when her mother took a step towards her.

"But Mom, those dishes weren't in there. I made sure the entire house was clean before you come home," Sharnese cried already seeing the outcome of the situation.

"So, you're calling me a liar?" Tonya yelled. Breathe reeking of alcohol. "You're just like your trifling ass father. Good for nothing. Can't-do shit right."

Sharnese was used to her mother's harsh words. Tonya was a scorned woman. She hadn't been the same since Corey, Sharnese's father left her when she was eight months pregnant.

Corey was Tonya's first love, high school sweetheart, her everything. Everything she did revolved around him. Corey was what you would call a lady's man. Mixed with Dominican and black. He had jet black curly hair, piercing grey eyes, and smooth skin the shade of butter pecan. It didn't help that the women loved his tall, 6'5" frame. But of course, with him being a lady's man came the extra attention from the side-chicks. Corey knew his attractiveness caught the eyes of many women and he used it to his advantage. He preyed on the weak and took over their minds. Plain and simple, Corey couldn't keep his dick in his pants. Somehow, he always ended up in random pussy.

Tonya stared at her daughter as her mind drifted back to the day that changed her mind forever.

The cold winter breeze smacked Tonya in her face as she dialed Corey's numb for the fifth time in a row. He was supposed to have been to her job over an hour ago with her car. After calling his phone and being sent to the voicemail she was left with no choice but to walk home.

"I can't believe this nigga not answering his damn phone. Got my ass walking in this freezing cold weather. His ass better have a good excuse. The way I'm feeling Jesus won't be able to save him

from my wrath. I'ma light his ass up like a firecracker on the fourth of July." Tonya fussed and cussed all the way to her house. She grew livid when she saw her black 1989 Acura Integra parked in the driveway. Opening the front door, she immediately senses that something isn't right.

Tonya looked down at the floor and spots a pink-lace thing, that she knows isn't hers. Slowly, she makes her way towards the back of the house and notices that her bedroom door is closed. "Why the hell is my bedroom door closed." She says to herself. Heart pounding, fearing the worst. She quietly places her hand on the doorknob. Taking a deep breath, she twists the knob and opens the door. What she sees next crushes her soul.

"That's right, suck this dick," Corey tells the red-headed jumpoff down on her knees as she deep throats him. With his eyes closed and hands behind his head. He enjoys the pleasure he's receiving.

Tonya eases her way into the bedroom and grabs the pink lamp from off the nightstand. Without thinking twice, she charges towards the red-headed girl and goes to work. Smashing the lamp into her head, blood gushes out everywhere. She continues into a fit of rage. Not quite satisfied with the results. She then begins to stomp the girl out on the floor until she's balled up into a fetal position covered in blood. Moving on to her next victim. She charges towards Corey. Tears cloud her vision as she starts swinging her arms, not sure if she's even hitting her target.

"How could you do this to me?" Tonya screamed. She charges towards him again. This time delivering a blow to his face. "After everything I've done for you, you bring some random bitch into our home. In the bed, we share together. Here I am, eight months pregnant with your child and you got me walking home from work in this cold weather while your laid back getting your dick sucked."

Ashamed of his actions, more so embarrassed for getting caught. Corey whispers, "I'm sorry Tee. I know I've fucked up this time."

"That's all you have to say is you're sorry? You damn right you're sorry. A sorry ass piece of an excuse for a man," Tonya yelled throwing insults. "Why is it so hard for you to stay faithful? I don't even know why I'm even upset. It's not like you have a car or a damn job. The only thing you can do is give me a wet ass. Truth be told, I don't even need you for that. That's why they make vibrators and dildos. I get more pleasure off a rubber dick than I do from yours."

"You know what? I don't have to listen to this shit. This is one of the reasons why I cheat, because of your fucking mouth. If you sucked my dick as much as you run your damn mouth then maybe I wouldn't cheat."

Tears continue to fall from Tonya's eyes. She couldn't believe the man she loved was speaking to her this way. He had never spoken to her in such a manner. Yes, she had slacked off with pleasing him in the bedroom, but with her protruding belly and constant morning sickness. It was impossible for her to engage in any kind of sexual activity comfortably. Still, that didn't give him an excuse to bring women into the home they shared together to cheat.

"I'm leaving," Corey said as he walked over to see if the red-headed chick named Tahiry was okay. "We're over. Now I can what I please and not have to worry about you bitchin' in my ear."

"But what about the baby? You know she could come any day now," Tonya cried.

"I don't even know if that baby is mine. Until I see a DNA test, I have no responsibilities as a father."

Those were the last words Tonya heard Corey say as he walked out the door and out of their lives forever. That same night, January 11th, at 11:58 P.M. she gave birth to a 5lb. 7oz. baby girl that she named Sharnese Jackson. Looking like the spitting image of her father.

At first, Tonya was the perfect mother, but as Sharnese grows older she begins to resemble her father even more. Tonya was constantly reminded of the heartache and pain she felt from Corey leaving her, so, alcohol became her remedy for mending her broken heart. Only it caused her more pain, instead of healing.

Sharnese sniffles snap Tonya back into reality.

"I'm sorry, Mom," Sharnese cried.

"You're damn right, you're sorry. You ain't never going to amount to shit," slurred a drunk Tonya.

Sharnese rolled her eyes. She was tired of her mother's negative words. For the first time ever, she was ready to stand up to her mother. Not caring about the physical abuse she would endure.

"It's not my fault my father left you. So you can stop making me pay for his mistakes." Sharnese screamed.

Smack!

Sharnese felt the hot, stinging vibration of her mother's hand burning against her face.

"I don't know who the hell you think you're screaming at, but there's only one head bitch in charge and that's me." Still fuming, Tonya grabs a handful of Sharnese's hair, knocking her down to the floor. She then drags her into the kitchen and picks up the wooden broom. She begins to beat her daughter as if she's a stranger on the street. Sharnese's beautiful brown skin is now covered in black bruises.

A concerned neighbor hears the commotion and calls the police. When the police arrive they hear the cries coming from a battered Sharnese. After kicking the door in and wrestling Tonya down to the ground, she's placed in handcuffs. She is arrested for numerous accounts of child abuse and child endangerment. Sharnese is then placed in the care of her grandmother, Mama Peaches.

Chapter One

"Hold your head still before I mess around and poke you too hard with this needle," Sharnese said to her cousin Brooklyn as she sewed in her 28 inches of black Brazilian extensions.

"Yeah, I hear you. When are you going to bring ya ass down to the club to make some real money? I mean, your hands are nice when it comes to slaying a bitch hair, but don't you get tired of standing on your feet all day long, making chump change? Don't you want your own place and privacy?"

Brooklyn was right. Sharnese was tired of living under her grandmother's roof, but she couldn't fathom the thought of degrading her body for a bunch of random, perverted men.

"Just come down to the club tonight. Not to audition or anything. Just to check out the scene and get a feel of the atmosphere. It's really not as bad as you think."

Brooklyn was one of the top, leading performers down at the strip club *Dazzlin' Diamonds*. She had been dancing there since the age of sixteen, after dropping out of high school to care for her infant son. Now twenty-six with four kids and three different baby daddies, she was still working the pole. Brooklyn made it appear as she made most of her money dancing. Truth was, Brooklyn was a trick. Her money came from messing with any drug dealer, athlete, lawyer, police officer or anyone that had enough money to capture her attention. She would even fuck the Pastor in the pulpit of the church if the offering money was right.

Brooklyn was the true definition of a bad bitch. She had smooth peanut butter colored skin that glows naturally. Her chinky eyes hypnotized any man who came in her presence. Many people often mistook her for having Asian in her blood. She stood at 5’7”, with 32DD breasts, and an ass that put Nicki Minaj to shame. Most women were intimidated by her beauty and the men didn’t trust her. They knew all about her scheming ways. Brooklyn wasn’t to be trusted and Sharnese would find out the hard way that blood wasn’t always thicker than water.

Finishing up Brooklyn’s hair, Sharnese grabs a mirror from off the wall and places it in front of her face. Brooklyn examines her hair thoroughly, making sure every strand is laid to perfection. “As usual you never let me down! I wish you would stop playing around and open up ya own shop already.” Brooklyn asked.

“Speaking of that, yesterday I enrolled into *Empire Beauty School*. I’m waiting to hear back from them so I can start,” Sharnese said as she took a sip of her wine.

“So, will I be seeing you at the club tonight?” Brooklyn asked while applying her MAC foundation to her face even though she could've done without it. Her skin was so flawless, not a pimple or blemish appeared on her face. Brooklyn knew she was the shit, and that was the exact reason she didn't have any friends.

"Stop pressuring that child into shaking her ass down at that club." Mama Peaches said as she walked into the kitchen to fix a glass of her famous lemonade. "Unlike you, she ain't about to sell her soul to the devil, just to buy a bunch of material things. Forgetting all about self-respect. No, she won't do it and I won't allow you to use her!" *Hmm, she must think I was born last night. Like I don't know she is down there selling her pussy to the highest bidder. I know all about the men my age that be having sex with my grand-daughter.* Mama Peaches just wanted Brooklyn to stop her ways before she either caught a disease or ended up in somebody's morgue due to her scheming ways finally catching up to her. She didn't want to have to bury a grandchild before she left this earth. They were supposed to bury her.

Word on the street was that an older Jamaican man by the name of Jean-Claude had a price out on Brooklyn's head. Apparently, she robbed him of forty-grand one night while they were in a hotel room. she was supposed to have been tricking with him, instead, she got greedy. While they were drinking, Brooklyn slipped an Ambien (sleeping pill) into his drink. Within minutes he was out cold and Brooklyn used that time to ransack his belongings. Brooklyn stole Jean-Claude's money to pay off his connect. Little did Brooklyn know. Not only did she make an enemy with him but also with the Shower Posse gang.

"Brooklyn baby, you really need to be careful. Especially with the lifestyle, you're living. The world is getting colder each day and people are getting more and more heartless. I'm not only saying this for your own good, but for the safety of your children. You don't even realize everything you do, not only puts yourself in danger but also your family. Remember that." Mama Peaches says as she walks out the kitchen.

"I hear everything that you're saying but that's still not going to stop me from getting money by any means necessary. Whether it's shaking my ass, selling it, robbing niggas or setting them up to be robbed. I'm a get this money!" Sharnese couldn't do anything but shake her head at her cousin's antics. She knew Brooklyn was dead serious about everything she had just said. "Hopefully I'll see you tonight. If not, it's no love lost boo." Brooklyn grabbed her three thousand dollar Gucci satchel and put on her oversized Chanel sunglasses to block her from the blazing sun that awaited her outdoors.

Realizing she hadn't spoken to her best friend all day. Sharnese goes to retrieve her iPhone 6 plus. Lying across her Queen-sized canopy bed she dials Destiny's number. After a few rings, she finally answers the phone. "Damn bitch, it took you long enough to pick up the phone," Sharnese said while painting her nails. "If you're busy. I can call you back later."

"You good, I was on the phone with Money. He wants to take a last minute trip to Jamaica this weekend. You should join us." Destiny said assuming Sharnese would say no like she always did.

"I could use a mini-vacation. It's been awhile since I've been able to unwind and enjoy myself. When we leaving?" asked an excited Sharnese.

"Friday morning. Make sure your ass is up and ready to go. That leaves you with two days to get your hair and nails done. Tomorrow afternoon we can go shopping." Destiny responded already thinking about how much she planned on spending.

"We can do that. That reminds me of why I called. If you don't have any plans, maybe you can hit up *Dazzlin' Diamonds* with me tonight."

Instantly Destiny caught an attitude. Her mood could go from zero to one hundred quick. Destiny was a straight hood chick. She looked exactly like the female rapper Trina except she was a tad bit thicker but her personality made her Remy Ma's twin. Despite being a hood chick, she had learned to control her emotions. She was on a full scholarship at one of the top law schools in New York. Her bar exam was only a few months away, and she refused to let anything stop her from completing it. Growing up in the hood she saw many black men receive long, lengthy sentences due to injustice and them not knowing the law. She was determined to help any criminal in the hood. Whether they were innocent or guilty.

"Don't that whore strip at that club?" Destiny sucked her teeth. "You know damn well I don't fuck with that bitch." Sharnese had forgotten all about the bad blood between Brooklyn and Destiny. The two women had one thing in common and his name was Money. Money was Destiny's boyfriend, but he also happened to share a five-year-old son with Brooklyn named Sincere. Whenever the two women were in each other's presence words were always exchanged. Which usually ended in them fighting.

"You're not going to support her. Think of it as a girls night out. If she even looks like she wants trouble then we can leave." Said Sharnese.

Destiny sighed. "I'll step out tonight with you. But if she looks like got a problem. I'm gonna fuck her up. Job or not."

"Alright, I'll be at ya crib around 10:30." Sharnese hung up the phone before Destiny could change her mind. Inside the bathroom, she filled the tub with her *Pure Seduction* shower gel. Her favorite fragrance from Victoria's Secret. With her hair wrapped, vanilla scented candles burning, and Marsha Ambrosius playing in the background. She's able to enjoy her bubble bath.

Before she knew it, an hour went by and she was still in the tub. Not sure as what she was going to wear. She looks in the closet and decides on a black cropped shirt, a plain pair of black shorts and her six-inch Red Bottoms. To make her outfit complete she puts on her gold bamboo hoops with her name in the middle. Satisfied with her attire for the night. She straightens her hair. Being mixed with Dominican and black, Sharnese had been blessed with long curly hair. Most days she let her natural locs run free, but tonight she wanted to let it hang.

Her hair and grey eyes along always seemed to get her into unwanted fights with jealous females. Back when she was in high school a group of girls picked on her constantly. It had never gotten physical until one of the girls named Monique, grabbed a handful of her hair and yanked it to see whether or not it was real. Before the girls could get another laugh out. Sharnese had sliced a four-inch cute on the right side of Monique's face with the razor she kept tucked under her tongue. Many of the bystanders stood around shocked. Some were frightened. It looked like a scene out of a horror movie. Blood was everywhere. Needless to say, Monique was left with a permanent scar. That day a point was made. Sharnese was not to be fucked with. Content with the results of her hair. She sprays on her favorite perfume *Tresor.* Grabbing her black Chanel tote bag and matching sunglasses she heads out the door to pick up Destiny.

Chapter Two

Sharnese didn't bother knocking on Destiny's door. When she walked into the apartment, Destiny was walking around in her birthday suit. They had been friends for so long, it was nothing for them to see each other naked.

"Well damn, I could've been a rapist coming through the door and you're in here with the door unlocked, prancing around with no clothes on."

"It ain't a nigga in this hood crazy enough to run up in here unwelcomed. Trust me when I tell you I have no problem sending shots to the head," Sharnese knew Destiny wasn't playing. She kept a loaded .45 on her always.

"Give me a few minutes to get dressed. I'll be right back."

Thirty minutes later Destiny stepped into the living room sporting a short, red bodycon dress with the back and sides out. It barely covered her ass. If she bent over every nigga in the club would have a clear view of her kitty. Making sure her hair was straight, they were on the way out the door. They chose to ride in

Destiny's 2013 Lincoln MKZ. Yes, Destiny was a hood bitch, but she prepared the finer things in life.

As they pulled up to the club they noticed it was super packed for it to be a weekday. There were no parking spaces and the line was starting to wrap around the building. Destiny shut the engine off and both ladies did a once over in the mirror before exiting the car. As soon as their feet hit the pavement, the comments from the thirsty men started.

"Damn shawty, what you trying to do? Make me have a heart attack," said some dark-skinned man with long dirty dreads and a bushy beard. "I know you gon let me hit tonight?" He grabbed Destiny's ass, only to find her pulling out her mace.

"Bitch, are you crazy? what the fuck is wrong with you?" He screamed in between breaths His eyes were on fire from Destiny spraying him in the face. Had they not been in public, Destiny would've shot his dick off for using the B-word. Yes, she joked around with her homegirls using that word but coming from a man it was considered as disrespect.

"The only bitch is ya mama for having ya stupid ass," Destiny responded rolling her eyes.

"Fuck you! I wasn't even trying to get at you for real. All these bitches around here. Sorry Ma, you aren't the baddest bitch walking. It ain't like ya pussy made of gold."

Destiny couldn't do anything but laugh. She was used to this kind of behavior from men she turned down. “Nigga you wish you could taste this golden pussy. I wouldn’t let you sniff the crack of my ass. Now getcha dirty, dusty ass the hell out of my face before shit gets real out here.” Embarrassed, the man quickly gets out of dodge.

“I can’t believe the nerve of that nigga. He grabbed my ass like he had money to pay for it. Both girls bust out laughing. They both know Destiny wasn't opening up her legs for anybody but Money. As they approached the door, they noticed the line had gotten a little shorter. The bouncer immediately recognizes Sharnese as Brooklyn’s cousin.

“What’s up? You Brooklyn’s cousin, right?”

“Yeah, why?” she replied with much attitude. Sharnese hated when people referred to her as being related to Brooklyn. For once she wanted people to know her as Sharnese Jackson.

“Chill Ma, no need for all the extra shit. I was just gonna let you and ya homegirl cut the line. That’s all.”

“Oh okay. I didn’t mean to come off that way. It’s just I… never mind.” Sharnese didn’t feel the need to explain herself. For all, she knows this could be a setup to start some drama between her and her cousin. Removing the velvet rope, he lets Sharnese and Destiny ahead. They hadn’t even made it inside before some dark-skinned chick with a busted weaved decided to start popping off at the mouth.

"I've been standing out here for damn near two hours. These bitches need to make their way to the back of the line."

Destiny wasn't in the mood for another altercation. They hadn't stepped foot inside the club and yet this was the second time someone felt the need to try her. Everyone was standing around waiting to see what was about to go down. For the girl's sake, she decided to proceed in the club but not before giving the girl a piece of her mind.

"Before you call yourself getting hype or whatever, you might want to take that cheap ass beauty supply hair out ya head. Nothing about that cheap ass Citi Trends outfit you're wearing is cute. Then you got the nerve to have on six-inch heels and you damn near seven feet tall looking a fucking mess." Destiny didn't give the girl a chance to respond as she went on about her business.

The pink and silver lights flashed throughout the entire room. *Dazzlin' Diamonds* wasn't any rundown strip club. Real diamonds boarded the Magenta colored walls. The entire floor was covered with plush black carpet. The carpet was so soft you could walk around with no shoes on. If you were caught inside, you had money. The bar consisted of nothing but expensive top-shelf liquor. The club required you to obtain a tab with a minimum of two hundred dollars to even sit at the bar.

The D.J. was on the mic getting ready to introduce the next dancer to shut down the stage. "Fellas, dig in ya pockets and grab them dollars. If you got plastic then I suggest you run to the ATM. Coming to the stage net is the club's top moneymaker, Paradise. If you're having girl problem then this ain't the place for you. This young lady is guaranteed to have you coming back for more."

In the locker room, Brooklyn was preparing to go on stage. Rubbing in the last of the baby oil on her body. She checked to make sure the little of her outfit was in place. It was something about big crowds that she loved, or it might have been the attention she craved. When she was on stage it felt like she was in another world. It was no longer about Brooklyn when she transformed into Paradise. The D.J. played Brooklyn's anthem *Flex by Mad Cobra.*

Girl flex, time to have sex

Look how long yuh have

Di rude bwoy a sweat

Girl flex, time to have sex

Look how long yuh have

Di rude bwoy a sweat

Brooklyn began gyrating her hips to the music. Dancing came naturally to her since she was flexible. Her long, slender legs made it easy to climb up and down the pole. Twirling around the pole, she dropped down into a full split and bounced her ass to the beat. When she does that the crowd instantly goes crazy. Men and women rush to the stage, making it rain big bills. Not quite finished with her performance just yet, she crawls towards a young man with long, neatly twisted dreads. Wrapping her legs tightly around his neck. She tightens her muscles and begins smoking the blunt he had in his mouth with her pussy.

Clouds of smoke form in the air and it sends the crowd into a frenzy. Flipping back over, she makes her ass clap in the man's face. When the music stops, she collects her money from the stage. On her way into the dressing room, she spots Sharnese sitting at the bar along with Destiny. Brooklyn could feel her blood beginning to boil. *Now, why the fuck would she bring this bitch here? Out of all fucking places, she brings the bitch to my place of employment. I don't give a fuck if this is a strip club. If she ain't throwing dollars at my ass, then she has no business being here. I should go slap that bitch. I already know one wrong move will fuck up any chances of her becoming a lawyer. Yup, that hoe needs to know she ain't the only one about that life.*

To Brooklyn, it wasn't even about the cash. Truth be told, Brooklyn was jealous of Destiny's relationship with Money. Brooklyn treated every nigga she became involved with as a potential trick. In return, that's exactly how Money ended up treating her. The only problem was Brooklyn ended up getting pregnant in the process. Smirking to herself, Brooklyn walks over to the bar. The only thing on her mind is getting under Destiny's skin. Brooklyn lived for this type of shit. She loved drama.

Chapter Three

Dej Loaf's, *Try Me Remix* blasted from out the club's surround system. Hearing her favorite song, hyped Brooklyn up. "Nese boo, you made it," Brooklyn said, totally ignoring Destiny's presence. "What are you drinking?" Sharnese orders a sex on the beach. "Better yet, order anything you want. Just put it on my tab. Brooklyn's favorite verse of the song comes on. She turns around and gives Destiny the meanest death stare ever while rapping the words to the song.

"Don't keep it in the stash, I keep it on me. Hit his wifey then his shawty. If one of these chicks ever try to try me. I'm a hit her whole muthafucking body!"

Sharnese shook her head already sensing it was about to go down. Destiny jumped up heated. She was trying to enjoy the night with her best friend. But no, Brooklyn just had to start some shit. Destiny couldn't risk catching an assault charge or possible murder charge behind a bitch that didn't want to go anywhere in life but on her knees. Thankfully, Destiny was good friends with the owner of the club, Ricky. Before Money came along, they shared a short fling. They both valued their friendship too much to mess it up in a relationship, so they called it off.

Destiny didn't want to bring any unwanted attention to his establishment, even though she knew if things got out of hand, he wouldn't call the police. The second level of the club was where the real money was made. It was set up exactly like a hotel. It consisted of ten rooms. Each with full bathrooms. Any and everything went down on the second floor.

"Bitch, if you got a problem let me know so we can get it popping. Bitches always claiming they bout that life until it's time to put in work," Destiny shouted.

Not wanting to be embarrassed at her job, Brooklyn knew she either had to put up or shut up! She takes her hand and mushes Destiny in her face. All hell breaks loose! Destiny grabs the nearest liquor bottle and smashes it against Brooklyn's head. Not fazed, Brooklyn grabs Destiny's hair and punches her in the face non-stop. The bouncer comes running to break up the fight.

"Cut this shit out now!" The bouncer snatches Destiny up and puts her over his big broad shoulders. If he had to put his money on the matter he would've guessed Brooklyn started the shit. Everybody that worked at or came to the club knew how she got down. If drama was unfolding. Brooklyn was either involved in it or not far from it. Although, he wanted to see Brooklyn get her ass whipped. He knew he had to remain professional or else Ricky will be on his ass.

"Bitch, you got that one. I'll give it to you, but guess what? I still got Money. I don't give a fuck about you two having a child together. I got something you'll never have and that's his heart! Every time you think in ya head that you stand a chance. You better think about the way my pussy tastes since he eats it for dinner every night! I see why he didn't wife ya trifling ass. You fucked him on the first night and didn't get anything out the deal but a child. It took him four months before he got anything out of me and guess what? The shopping sprees, vacations and cars came instantly. I'll always have one up on you!"

Deep inside, Brooklyn knew Destiny was telling nothing but the truth. She didn't have Money's heart and that was something she wanted badly. Her love for cash made it impossible for her to love no matter how hard she tried. She was too blinded by the material things to even notice when a person was being genuine. The words Destiny spoke hurt Brooklyn deep, but she refused to let her know that. Always one to have the last laugh. Brooklyn says the first thing that comes to her mind.

"You may have his heart, but he's still playing on my team. Always have and always will. Now, don't you ever forget that! Don't look so sad baby girl. Pick ya face up," Brooklyn said as she walked off.

"Bitch it's not over! You better believe that shit!" Destiny yelled. *That bitch better sleep with both eyes open. Not only is she going to pay for getting me out of character but for bringing up Money's name.* Every bitch in the hood knew not to mention Money's name around Destiny. That was automatic grounds for an ass whipping. Destiny was getting tired of Brooklyn thinking she could get away with disrespecting her. Destiny also knew it was part of the game. Especially when dealing with a nigga who had an ignorant baby mama who wasn't over them.

It was obvious Brooklyn still had feelings for Money. Why else was she always fucking with her? But the question that lingered in Destiny's mind wondered whether or not Money was still fucking with Brooklyn. Not once had she ever thought Money was cheating on her, but after fighting with Brooklyn it made her wonder. She was definitely going to get her answers once she gets home.

Sharnese runs to Destiny's side. "Oh my god, Des are you alright? I feel like this is my fault. I should've never kept pressuring you to come out. I'm so sorry."

"It's alright Nese. Let's just leave before things get out of hand again. Are you hungry?"

"Yeah, I could go for a bite to eat."

"Let's go then."

Chapter Four

In the locker room, Brooklyn was laughing, cutting up with a few of the girls that worked at the club about the fight between her and Destiny.

"Brooklyn, you were dead wrong," said Fantasy. "Shawty was just chilling at the bar minding her business. As usual, you find somebody to fuck with. Keep on, one of these days you gon meet ya match." Fantasy hated how always found a way to start drama with innocent people. She couldn't wait until the day karma finally bit her in the ass. Just a Brooklyn was about to respond, Ricky, the club's owner, came barging through the door. Everyone could sense some shit was about to go down. He rarely made an appearance in the locker room.

"Everybody except Paradise, get out now!" The girls continue with their business. They were used to Ricky being loud, so they paid him no mind.

"Okay, I see y'all think it's a game. If y'all aren't out of here within the next five seconds, every one of you bitches will be suspended for the next five days!"

One by one the girls rush out the locker room. The weekend was coming up and none of them wanted to miss out on the cash that was sure to be flooding the club. All the dope boys, rappers, and athletes came through on the weekends. For Ricky to be talking about suspending his dancers for five days, then he was pissed off about something. Sensing his attitude was about her, Brooklyn tries to ease her way out the door. Ricky stops her dead in her tracks.

"Just where the hell do you think your ass is going, Paradise?" Ricky calls Brooklyn by her stage name. "Get ya ass in here and close the damn door! What the fuck happened out there? I'm sick of your as thinking you can do whatever the hell you want and not have to suffer any consequences. You may bring in a lot of money, but you aren't any different from the rest of the girls. You will obey the rules around here, or else you're gonna find yourself selling ya ass on the streets. Fighting will not be tolerated. Keep that shit in the streets!" Ricky had just said a mouthful, not once stopping to let Brooklyn say a word. "Now do we have an understanding?"

"Yes, Ricky." Brooklyn was not about to waste her time arguing with him. It was bad enough she was talking to him, missing out on making money. Unbuckling his pants, Ricky lets loose his nine-inch anaconda. Staring at Brooklyn's chocolate nipples, he stroked his dick up and down making it hard. Licking her lips, Brooklyn spreads open her legs. Raising one leg in the air. She gives him a full view of her neatly shaven pussy. Using her fingers,

Brooklyn massages her clit. Ricky walks over towards her and on cue Brooklyn flips over on all fours and toots her ass in the air.

Brooklyn couldn't wait to feel Ricky inside of her. It had been awhile since the two of them had messed around. His dick game was so vicious, he could make a stud turn straight again. If any female that had been with him said they didn't have an orgasm. It was either a lie, or her pussy had been ran through so much, she didn't have any walls. With Ricky's rock-hard dick pressed against her ass. Brooklyn lets a quiet moan slip out of her mouth.

"Mmm, daddy don't tease me. Go ahead and put it in. I want to feel every inch of you inside me. Grabbing Brooklyn's hips tightly he slides his dick in as soon as he enters her from behind. He feels himself about to cum already.

Damn Paradise, you're nice and tight just the way I like it." Hearing those words, she gets wetter. Her juices start flooding all over Ricky's dick. Feeling his balls slap against the back of her kitty, she reaches under and begins massaging them. Ricky could feel the head of his shaft begging to swell. Each thrust he gives causes her ass to shake like an earthquake.

"Oh shit, I'm about to nut." He pulls out releasing his seeds all over her backside. Brooklyn grabs some baby wipes from out of her bag and begins cleaning herself up. "Paradise, your pussy was good and all, but you're suspended until Monday," Ricky says as he pulls his pants up.

"What did you just say?"

"You heard right. You're suspended until the weekend is over. You can start your suspension as soon as you're dressed." Brooklyn couldn't believe what her ears were hearing.

"How the fuck is you going to suspend me? I'm the bitch that makes the most money in this muthafucka!" she hollered.

"That is true. You do make the most money in here, but you're going to learn to follow the rules around here. I don't give a fuck how much money you bring in here. You can be replaced with another dancer, with the stunt you pulled. Somebody could've easily called the police and had the club shut down. It's too many illegal activities going on here to have that kind of attention drawn to us."

Pissed didn't even describe how Brooklyn felt. "You know what? Fuck you!" Brooklyn began throwing all her belongings inside of her pink and black zebra printed suitcase. "Ya dick was whack, straight garbage. Each moan you thought you heard was fake. Don't you know I'm a master when it comes to running games? It's levels to this shit when it comes to fucking with a boss bitch like me!"

Furious, she slams the door on her way out. Leaning up against the wall, she takes a deep breath to get herself together. She already knew bitches were going to be wondering what had taken place between her and Ricky. Feeling confident, she struts onto the floor making her way to the exit. Brooklyn stops walking when she notices the smirk the bouncer has on his face as she approaches the door.

"The fuck you smirking at? Move ya fat, greasy ass up out my way before you end up being my next victim." The smirk that resided on his face quickly faded away. He didn't want to be next on her list. There was no telling how far she was willing to go to seek her revenge on anybody she felt crossed her.

Once outside, Brooklyn walks to her silver Lexus ES with twenty-four-inch chrome rims. An eerie feeling came over her. She felt as if someone was watching her. Brooklyn stopped walking and checked her surroundings. Seeing nothing unusual, she picks up her pace and continues walking to her car.

Pop! Pop! Pop! Pop!

Brooklyn drops down to the ground immediately. The whole time her mind was wondering who could be shooting at her. It was no telling who the culprit could have been since she had so many enemies in the streets. Brooklyn spots an all-black Cadillac Escalade speeding out of the parking lot. She had never seen the SUV before a day in her life. She made sure to keep a mental note of it in her head. Slowly, she gets up from the ground. With her hands shaking, she attempts to take off her heels and makes a run for her car.

Pop! Pop! Pop! Pop!

Now she was certain her name was written on those bullets. The glass shattered everywhere as the bullets fired holes into the windows of another man's vehicle. You would've thought someone was handing out free cash the way people were running out the club to spectate.

This time an all-white van with no windows drives off in the night. A frantic Brooklyn struggles to regain her composure. She couldn't believe how close she was to having her life taken away. Her hands shook violently as she tried to pull her keys out her purse. Brooklyn was a nervous wreck. The bouncer from inside the club walks over to see if she's alright.

"Paradise, you good?" he asked.

She wanted to say hell no, Instead, she responded with a simple "Yeah, I'm good," Brooklyn put on a fake smile and walked to her car.

Chapter Five

It was three-thirty in the morning and the girls were still sitting inside of *Waffle House* stuffing their faces.

"Are you going to ask Money about the shit Brooklyn said?" Sharnese asked Destiny whole taking a bite of her steak. It was so juicy and tender, the only thing it was missing was a dab of A1 steak sauce.

"You damn right I'm going to ask his ass. I don't care if the bitch is lying. When it comes down to my man you already know I don't play games. She lucky I didn't really get to mop the floor with her dumb ass like I wanted to. The mother of his child or not, she will respect me!"

Destiny took a sip of her water to calm her nerves. She was still pissed at herself for even allowing Brooklyn to get her out of character. One wrong move could mess up everything she had worked so hard for. Glancing at her phone she sees it's going on five o'clock in the morning. They had been there for damn near two hours. They had the waiter pack up the rest of their food to go. Thirty minutes later they were back at Destiny's apartment. They pull into the driveway beside Money's red Cadillac DTS. The lights were on which meant he was still up.

"I can't believe he's even here. Any other time he would still be on the block until the sun came up."

"Well, I would take it as a good thing. Especially since he's home this time of morning and not running the streets."

"I guess you're right. What time you wanna meet up to go shopping?"

"Around three. That's enough time to get some sleep and be ready."

"Alright girl, I'll you in the afternoon."

Sharnese got into her car and drove off. Destiny walked into the house to find Money laid back on the chocolate leather sectional watching old episodes of *Love & Hip-Hop New York*. Destiny curls up under him on the sofa. Money bends down to give her a kiss and jumps up yelling.

"What the fuck happened to ya damn face?" Destiny never thought to look and see what type of marks Brooklyn left on her face. She jumps up off the sectional and runs into the bathroom. Examining her face in the mirror. She sees a long, red scratch underneath her eye. *Damn, that bitch got me good.* Opening the medicine cabinet, she takes out the rubbing alcohol, peroxide and some cotton balls. The burning sensation of the alcohol causes her heart to pound. She walks back into the living room to explain the incident that occurred earlier. A long sigh escapes her lips.

"Your ignorant ass baby mama is what happened. That bitch popped off in the club and mushed me in my damn face! She lucky I ain't have my burner on me or else Sincere would be motherless right now. Money, I'm sick of this bitch. Every time she sees me in public, she's constantly fucking with me. I swear if I wasn't so close to completing my bar exam, her ass would've been six feet under a long time ago. So, either you handle the situation or I'm going to handle it my way."

Money knew that if he let Destiny handle the situation Brooklyn would most likely come up floating in the Hudson River. As much as he hated his baby mama, he didn't want to see his son grow up without a mother.

"That leaves me with this question. Are you still fucking Brooklyn?" Money looked at Destiny in disbelief. He couldn't believe that she had just asked him that dumb shit.

"Come on now Des, you know better than to ask me some dumb shit like that. But to answer your question No, I'm not fucking Brooklyn. Shit, it's been so long I couldn't tell you the last time I fuck her. You know I would never jeopardize what we've built."

One thing about Money was that he always kept it one hundred with Destiny. He had never once cheated on her or even though about it for that matter. Most niggas were fascinated with fucking a million bitches and keeping a couple of side chicks. Not him though, Money just wanted to make money so that he could eventually get out the streets, and start a family. He planned on proposing to Destiny while they were in Jamaica. He knew she could use the trip to take her mind off school.

Destiny had been with him since the beginning. Back when he was dirt broke and fucked up. She never made him feel like he was nothing. If anything, she encouraged him to do better. She had even given him the money to buy his first package. The only thing she asked in return was for his loyalty, to keep it one hundred with her at all time, and to never cheat.

Those were simple things to Money. When he did start getting money he spoiled her with anything she asked for. Not only did she fuck with him the long way. She was an excellent mother figure to his son. She treated him just as if he were her own. That alone made Money want to wife her. Even though she was a hood chick, she never once showed that side in front of his son.

Examining the scar on Destiny's face, Money became infuriated. His mind was telling him to go fuck Brooklyn up personally, but he had to be careful about approaching her. You never knew what Brooklyn had going on in her head and he didn't want to risk getting into any trouble with the law. He had never been in any trouble, not even a warning for a speeding ticket and he wanted to keep it that way.

"Don't worry baby, I'm going to handle this situation. Go ahead and get some rest. You're going to need it for this weekend," He placed ten stacks onto the chocolate and tan marbled coffee table. "Take this and go shopping. Let me know if you need more," grinning from ear to ear, he reaches over and kisses him on the kips.

"Thanks, baby, I doubt I'll even spend all of this."

She was happy about the money he had given her. Now she could take her money and put it back in her stash. The sun was starting to shine through the blinds. Looking at the clock she saw it was already going on seven in the morning. She walked into her bedroom ready for bed. In her case a nap. She strips out of her bloodstained clothes and throws them into the corner. Tying her scarf around her hair she hops in the shower and scrubs away any dried-up blood that remained on her body. Letting the hot water surface over her, she feels her muscles loosen up. Drying off and popping two Tylenol extra strength pills into her mouth and climbs into bed, praying that her body wouldn't be sore from the fight.

Destiny wakes up to the sound of her phone vibrating on the nightstand. Looking at the caller I.D. she sees its Sharnese calling. She had forgotten all about the plans they made to go shopping. After the third ring, she finally answers the phone.

"Hello?"

"I know damn well ya ass ain't still in bed. Was the dick that good that it put ya ass in a coma?" Sharnese laughed.

"I see you got jokes this morning."

"It's almost four o' clock in the afternoon, and you haven't left yet? How you are feeling though?"

"Besides this ugly scratch under my eye, I'm good. I popped a couple pills before I went to bed. That took away most of the pain. Now Money, on the other hand, is pissed. He didn't say a lot on the matter, but from his body language, I could tell that he wanted to go kill up the world. You know I confronted him about if he was still fucking with Brooklyn."

"What did he say? I bet her ass was lying to get under your skin."

"You already know she was."

"Damn, I knew it. Jealously is an ugly trait. That's my cousin and all, but if she wasn't always plotting to rob niggas of their money then maybe they would fuck with her. These niggas will fuck her, but they won't fuck with her."

"We've been on this phone long enough. Meet me at Sak's on 611 5th street in one hour."

"Alright, I'll see you there."

Chapter Six

After two hours of shopping, Sharnese and Destiny had more than enough outfits to take with them on their vacation. The sales girl smiled at the total price. More so, she was smiling at the commission she had made. Together they spend around four-thousand dollars which weren't bad compared to what they normally spent.

Brooklyn had been calling Sharnese's phone all day. Sharnese ignored her calls, figuring Brooklyn was calling to brag about the drama she had started the night before. Each time she called, she sent it straight to the voicemail. Brooklyn was really calling to inform her of the shooting that had occurred. Once the girls parted their separate ways, they both head home to start packing. Double-checking her bags to make sure she wasn't forgetting anything, Sharnese loads her luggage into her car.

"Going somewhere, baby?" Mama Peaches asked just as Sharnese was walking back into the house.

"Yeah, I'm going on a mini vacation to Jamaica this weekend with Destiny. After everything that has happened this week, I could use a break from being around here," Mama Peaches frowns her face.

“Chile, what nonsense done took place around here that Mama Peaches don’t know about?”

Sharnese let out a long sigh. She knew Mama Peaches wasn’t too fond of Brooklyn and her ways. Now she was wishing she never opened her mouth. Sharnese thought long and hard about what to say next. She was hoping Mama Peaches changed the subject, but it would never happen. Once you said anything to Mama Peaches, she turned into the FBI. She would interrogate you to the point where you could feel the energy leave your body. It was like she could look inside of you and tell when you were lying or trying to cover something up.

“Nothing major. Just the drama that normally takes place in the hood.”

“I see. Whenever you freeze you freeze up like that I can almost bet it has something to do with the one and only Miss Brooklyn.” Fidgeting with her hands, Sharnese looks down at the tiles on the kitchen floor.

“I got to finish packing,” she says as she tries to move past her, but Mama Peaches was standing in her way.

“Your ass ain’t going nowhere until you tell me what the hell your damn cousin done did now! Sharnese Jackson, don’t play with me,” Mama Peaches rarely cursed at Sharnese, but whenever Brooklyn’s name was mentioned it changed her mood. More than likely Brooklyn was in some shit. Sharnese tells Mama Peaches about the fight between Destiny and Brooklyn.

"Serves her ass right!" Mama Peaches grinned.

"Mama Peaches, that's your grand-daughter you're talking about!"

"That may be true. I'm just sick of her walking around here like her shit doesn't stink. Let me guess, they were fighting over Sincere's father?" Shaking her head Mama Peaches takes a sip of her lemonade. "That body don't want no damn Brooklyn. She had her chance but she was too stuck in her whorish ways."

"That's not nice."

"Chile, I'm just keeping it what you kid say…one hundred." Sharnese laughed. Mama Peaches stayed trying to keep up with the latest slang. A few times Sharnese had caught her using words that she hadn't even started using. She had even walked in on her twerking a few times.

Mama Peaches aged like wine. She got finer over time. If you were to see her you would never believe she was fifty-nine years old. Her appearance hadn't changed much at all. She didn't look a day over thirty-five. She had a body that would put a lot of twenty-year-olds to shame. She kept her honey blonde hair cut in a shoulder length bob with Chinese bangs, and she stayed rocking the latest fashion trends. You can only imagine how Sharnese felt seeing her grandma rocking a body-con dress and red bottoms. Sharnese didn't know much about Mama Peaches in her younger days except she had her mom and aunt at an early age. The way she acted now often made her wonder what type of lifestyle she lived back in the day. She also wondered if it was the reason she hated Brooklyn's scheming ways so much. Sharnese just didn't know that in time Mama Peaches hidden past would soon be revealed.

"You see Baby, your cousin is going to wind up getting herself into some shit that nobody is going to be able to get her out of. I just don't want you caught in the middle. I know this may sound a bit harsh, but you aren't built for the type of lifestyle Brooklyn is involved in. Your heart is too soft. People will use that and take advantage of you. In this world, always remember to go with your first instinct. If you feel a situation ain't right, then listen to it. Brooklyn is a lost soul. I don't know if anything can change her ways, but you're a different story. I see the potential you have in you. Don't fall victim to these streets."

Sharnese let what Mama Peaches just said marinate in her head. Even though Mama Peaches was right, Sharnese felt like she and Brooklyn had a connection that no one would ever understand. Not only was she her first cousin, she was also the sister she never had. Being the only child, Sharnese had no siblings to look up to, and that's where Brooklyn came into play

"Mama Peaches, Can I ask you a question?"

"Now you know you can ask me anything."

"How come you never talk about your younger days? We really don't know much about your past," Mama Peaches wanted so badly to tell Sharnese about her past, but she just couldn't bring herself to do so.

"Baby, the timing just isn't right, but one day I will reveal it all, one day," Hearing those last words made Sharnese raise her eyebrows. She was now even more suspicious of her grandmother's past.

"On another note. I want you to enjoy yourself. I also want you to do me a favor."

"You know I'd do anything for you."

"Please find yourself a man," Sharnese turns red from embarrassment. Was it that obvious that she had no love life? There were always men trying to get at her, but she always turned them down. She knew her self-worth. Most of them just wanted to have sex with her. They saw her ass and not her assets. She didn't want to be just a quick fuck that left her being a side-chick or baby mama. She wanted a King to treat her like the Queen she was. Somebody to spoil her with all the things in life she deserved. Sharnese wanted it all. Not the material things but the love, loyalty, and respect. She wanted somebody she could build with. Somebody who fucked with her the same way she fucked with them. A man that would have her back when times get rough. He didn't have to have money, she could finance herself. More than anything, one day she wanted to start a family of her own and be able to give her child the love she never received growing up.

"Now grandma, I don't be all up in your business. Don't be in mines," Sharnese runs to her bedroom and closes her door before Mama Peaches can respond. She could be a piece of work at times.

Standing in front of her floor-length mirror, Sharnese admires the big Poetic Justice braids she's wearing. Normally she would never rock braids. She felt braids were for kids, but who wanted to do their hair while on vacation? She didn't. Realizing her and Destiny never discussed where they were going to meet in the morning, she sends her a text.

Sharnese: Where are we meeting?

Destiny: JFK airport. Leave early to be the traffic.

Sharnese: Okay, see you then.

Chapter Seven

Brooklyn paced her living room floor nervously, peeking out the blinds every five minutes. Paranoid from being shot at, she was constantly looking over her shoulder to see if someone was following her. So far nothing seemed out of the ordinary, but to be on the safe side she went and purchased herself a gun. Luckily for her, it was the summertime and the kids were down South visiting her Aunt Caroline. Brooklyn tried calling Sharnese's phone but all she got was the voicemail.

"Ahh!" she screamed. There was nobody she could call since she had no friends. Too petrified to leave the house. She turns on her favorite movie *Shottas* and orders some Chinese food. Wanting to take her mind off everything, she grabs her weed from out of the ashtray.

A knock on the door interrupts her smoke session. When she opens the door, there's no one there. Walking outside she steps on a yellow manila envelope. "What the fuck is this? Hopefully, it's some U.S. currency inside," she says out loud to herself. Once back inside the house, she empties the content from the envelope and lets out a horrifying scream.

On the floor lays a silver machete with she thinks appears to be someone or something's dried up blood. Tears begin to flood her eyes. Whoever was behind the shooting knew where she laid her head. Brooklyn rushes to her room immediately and grabs the duffel bag with the money she had stolen from Jean-Claude. Making sure her gun is off the safety, she opens the front door and there stands a man dressed in all-black wearing a ski mask. The unknown man lunges his hand towards her throat. His tight grip makes it impossible for her to breathe.

Slowly Brooklyn felt her life slipping away from her body but being the fighter, she is, it wasn't going to be that easy to take her away from here. *How the fuck am I going to get away from this me? Better yet who the fuck is he and who sent him?* A million and one questions raced through her mind. With the little strength she has left, she raises her left knee as high as it'll go and knees the man in her private area. Caught off guard, he falls to the ground and releases his hand from her neck.

"Weh de blood clot!" he yells as he hits the floors. Brooklyn pulls out her gun and aims it at his head.

"Who sent you?" she says frantically wanting to know who was out to kill her.

"I'm nah tell yuh dodo." From his strong accents and the words he spoke, Brooklyn could instantly tell he was Jamaican.

From only having personal dealing with one Jamaican man she knew then who was after her.

"Jean Claude sent you, didn't he?" The man laughed in Brooklyn's face.

"To rass!"

Tired of playing games. She fires three shots into his skull. Brooklyn watches as his blood and brain matter splatter over the door. It takes a couple of seconds for her to register that she killed someone for the first time. *Better him than me,* she thought. Not sure of what to do next. Brooklyn grabs her keys, the duffel bag and makes a run to her car. Backing up into the mailbox and running over a trashcan, she drives out the yard. *Where the hell am I going to go now? I could go to Mama Peaches house, but then she'll see the bruise on my neck and start asking a bunch of damn questions. I am not in the mood to listen to her mouth.*

Out of nowhere a cop car pulls up behind her. Sweat begins to exude on her forehead. Blue and red lights appear from the car. Brooklyn pulls off on side of the road. Luckily for her, he speeds past her, paying her no mind. *Thank you, Jesus, that was a close one.* Brooklyn wasn't a religious person, but at that moment he had to have been looking out for her. With nowhere to go, she drives until her body is exhausted. Uncertain of where she's at, the sign ahead of her says Welcome to Atlantic City, New Jersey. Checking into a room at *Harrah's Resort* he throws her back into the closet and stretches out across the bed.

Chapter Eight

Everyone please fasten your seatbelts, and remain seated. You will be arriving at your destination in approximately ten minutes," said the flight attendant.

"Now where is Money at? He was supposed to be here already." Destiny grew frustrated as she looked around the airport looking for Money. He had arrived in Jamaica a day earlier to have a meeting with his connect. Just then, she spots him, but he wasn't alone. With him his homeboy Murda. She doesn't know a whole lot about him except that him and Money been doing business together for a few years.

"Hey baby," she greets him with a passionate kiss on his lips. Money embraces her with a hug while palming her ass.

"Sup Ma, I missed ya ass," The way they were kissing you would've thought they were auditioning for a scene in a movie.

"Um hello, we are still standing here. You two lovebirds have the next few days to play catch up," Sharnese said.

"Damn my fault Sis, how you been?" Money asks.

"I'm good, glad to be away for a while."

"I feel you on that."

"Well since you aren't going to introduce a nigga, looks like Ill introduce myself. What's up with you? I'm Murda," He extends his arm out for a handshake.

"Hmm, Murda. I know your mother didn't name you that. How about you introduce yourself using your government name," Sharnese looked at Murda with a straight face waiting for his response. Murda licked his lips and smiled. Already, he likes her aggressiveness. The vibe he got from her was different. He was used to dealing with females that never bothered asking his name. Their only focus was on how much money they could get from him.

"I apologize Ma, my name is Cortez."

"Well it's nice to meet you, Cortez, I'm Sharnese," she replied with a wide grin. Destiny and Money fall out laughing at the two of them.

"Alright nigga, stop trying to play love connection. We ready turn up. Y'all can do that shit on ya own time," Money grabs Destiny bags and attempt to flag down a taxi.

"Oh yeah, Nese I forgot to tell you that you and Murda will be sharing a suite together. Don't worry it has two bedrooms. You'll only be sharing the bathroom. Money and I are about to catch a cab to the resort. You can tag along with us or get to know your roommate," Destiny says seriously. Not even waiting for a response, Destiny jumps in the taxi with Money.

"Looks like it's just me and you. Don' t worry, I don't bite," Murda jokes. Sharnese smiles at his sense of humor. "We need to find a way to the resort. Can you speak Creole?"

"No, all I know is the good ol' American language."

"That shouldn't be a problem. I speak a couple different languages." Murda takes off towards a Jamaican man standing outside a cab. "Fi mon ou much fah ah ride?"

"Fah yuh ten dollars," Murda gives the man the address to the resort. In his best English, the man says "This is almost a two-hour ride. It'll cost more."

"Money ain't an issue," Murda pulls out a wad of cash. They dap each other up and begin loading the bags into the trunk. "Alright Ma, it's about a two-hour ride to the resort. We might as well make the best of it."

"Let's go," Sharnese smiles from ear to ear. For some strange reason, she felt comfortable around him. Sharnese goes to open the door but Murda stops her.

"What the fuck are you doing?" Caught off guard Sharnese becomes defensive.

"What the fuck does it look like I'm doing? I'm getting in the damn cab!"

"Look shawty, I don't know what type of niggas you're used to being around, but as long as you're in my presence you will never open your own door. Or any door for that matter. I was raised with manners."

Speechless Sharnese moves out the way so he can open the door. Once inside the cab, she turns to thank him and that's when she notices just how attractive he is. His hazel eyes had her stuck in a daze. By looking at his long braids and light complexion she can tell he's mixed with something. Sharnese could feel her panties getting moist. She wanted Murda bad. Even with the clothes he had on, you could tell he was in shape and not an ounce of fat appeared on his body. He made her want to do something right there in the backseat.

"Tell me a little about yourself, Miss Sharnese," Murda says.

"Ain't much to it, I'm 23, no kids, no man."

"Nah, it has to be more to you than just those things. Tell me about your past. Everyone has a story. I want to know your goals, dreams, what you want out of life," Sharnese lowers head. Murda sees the hurt and pain on her face. Immediately he regrets opening his mouth. "My bad Ma, you don't have to talk about it if you don't want to."

"You're okay. It's just I've never talked about it to anyone before," Silence feels the cab. Sharnese take a deep breath as she proceeds to relive her past. "Growing up I was abused both mentally and physically by my mother. My father left before I was born. I don't know much about him except that I look just like him. Long story short. My mother was a scorned woman who used alcohol to hide her pain, but instead, it released her anger. She would hit me with anything she got her hands on. One night she came home so drunk, she beat me with a wooden broomstick until my body was covered in blue and black bruises. Thankfully, a neighbor heard what was happening and called the police. Since then I've been living with my grandmother in Brooklyn."

"Damn," was all Murda could muster to say. By looking at Sharnese you would never know she had been through so much. Her smile alone could brighten an entire room.

"What are your goals? What do you do for a living?"

"As of right now, I'm in enrolled in Cosmetology school. Once I'm finished, I plan on opening a chain of salons across the world." Murda had to admit he was impressed. A lot of females did hair and opened beauty salons but you rarely heard of them wanting to have a franchise of salons.

"Enough about me. What do you do for a living? No offense, but you have a pair of $1200 Prada sneakers on your feet. An average person working a regular nine to five doesn't even bring that home after taxes." Under normal circumstances, he would never reveal how he made his money to a female he'd just met. Or to any female for that matter. Since he was feeling Sharnese he came clean.

"I'm a dope boy," he replied shrugging his shoulders like it was no big deal.

"So, you sell drugs?" she asked.

"Nah, I like to refer to myself as a Pharmaceutical Distributor."

"Wow! I've never heard anyone use that term before," they both fall out laughing.

"For real though, my father was a known big-time drug dealer/ pimp back in the day and my mom was his bottom bitch. They met when my mom was 16. She had run away from home at the time. Being young and naïve she fell into the arms of my father. Not knowing he was a pimp. At first, he had her tricking with different men until he broke the number one rule and caught feelings for her. Once that happened he pulled her out the stable and soon after I came along."

"Sound like their relationship was pretty interesting…." Sharnese joked. The view outside of the window was breathtaking. They were so high up on a mountain, Sharnese was sure they would tip over at any given moment. She glances over at Murda and catches him taking in the scenery. She grabs his braids and imagines the different type of styles she could come up with.

"Do you ever plan on getting out one day?" she asks out the blue. As much as Murda wanted to leave the streets alone. He knew it would never happen.

"This lifestyle is my way of living. I didn't get the name Murda just because it sounds good. I done made a lot of enemies. Even if I did get out I would still have to watch my back," Sharnese had more questions she wanted to ask, but she didn't want to ruin the mood.

"Why don't you have a man? You seem like a nice girl and all. You're fine as hell so why are you single?" Sharnese thought long and hard about how she should respond to his questions. She didn't want to sound stuck up.

"Well for one, most niggas just want to fuck. I'm worth more than someone's quick fuck. I want a real relationship. I don't have time for games, baby mamas, side chicks or none of that extra stuff. For real, I'm just trying to stack my dough and get on my feet."

For a minute Murda was left speechless. For the first in his life, he had finally found a girl who wasn't concerned with how much money he had. He knew women much older than her who didn't have their shit together. Already Sharnese was a keeper and she didn't know it. Murda could see them building an empire together. He could tell she was about her business and that's the kind of woman he needed on his team.

"On some real shit, I just met you like five minutes ago, but I'm really feeling you. It takes a lot to capture my attention, and you had me when you asked for my real name. If you were any other female I would've been certain you were working with the police. Plain and simple, I'm trying to make you my girl. There's ya invitation, let me know when you're ready to reserve your spot."

Sharnese couldn't respond. She was stuck and didn't know what to say. *Damn, I wasn't expecting this nigga to come at me like this. Hell, we just met and already he wants to make it official. Where's Ashton Kutcher? I feel like I'm being punked.* So many thoughts consumed Sharnese's mind. Running her fingers through her braids she thinks long and hard.

"Well, I guess we in this together."

Murda smiled. He was sure she was going to turn him down. Most chicks would've thought he was crazy for putting everything on the table like that. He just wanted her to know he was being sincere.

"Wi will be dere in one minute," the driver said as they approached the resort.

Chapter Nine

The view from the car was magnificent. Several different shades of blue absorbed the Caribbean waters. Destiny couldn't stop herself from taking her sandals off and running her feet through the sand. It wasn't the kind of sand you saw on the beaches back in the states. The sand in Jamaica was white and soft as cotton. You couldn't feel not one rough spot. Even with the sun beaming, it couldn't burn you.

"Well look who finally decided to join us," Destiny struts over sporting a long, thin Maxi sundress, with a huge straw hat. "Sorry I left you, Nese, I had some catching up to do with my man."

"Yeah, you had some catching up to do alright. More like you had ya ass totted up getting dicked down," Destiny rolled her eyes and stuck her tongue out at Sharnese.

"See that's where you're wrong. I bounce up and down on the dick! Did you enjoy the long drive up?"

"Yeah, actually I did. Murda pretty much asked me to be his girl."

"Say what? I don't know how you managed to pull that one. Do you know how hard it is to catch his attention? I hope you're ready for everything that comes along with being his girl. He ain't no average nigga. He's straight boss status. Bitches would kill to be in ya position. My best friend done moved on up in the world. I can't believe your finally dating. Wait until Mama Peaches hear about this," Destiny laughed.

"Shit, before I left she told me to find a man. I really feel like he could be the one. For once in my life, I'm ready to be happy and do what pleases me. All my life I've felt like I was worth nothing because of the way my mother treated me. Now I've met someone who makes me feel special. I know I've only known him for a few minutes but it seems like forever."

"If you're happy, then I'm happy for you. Now let's go find our men before we have to beat some Jamaican ass. You know these island bitches are some straight freaks. I would hate to catch a case in unknown territory. Mess around and they have our asses hidden in somebody's mountains being sex slaves."

Sharnese frowns her face while shaking her head. "Where do you get this type of shit form?"

"Girl T.V., have you not seen the show *Dateline*? All types of crazy shit be happening to people when they go on trips to foreign countries. I'm not trying to be gang-raped by a bunch of Jamaican men with Mandingo dicks. You know they be packing."

"You know what, I'm done with you. I'm ready to explore the island, and get some of this good Caribbean food." The girls find men at the bar taking shots of Vanilla Rum. Money waves the bartender down for another shot. He wasn't a heavy drinker, but he had just bet Murda three hundred dollars that he could outdrink him and there was no way he was about to lose out on free dough.

"This shit here ain't nothing like that watered-down stuff we be drinking on back home. This is the real deal." Money didn't know how many drinks he would be able to handle so he ordered some jerk chicken and white rice to help sober him up. it was still early in the day and he knew Destiny would be pissed if he messed around and got drunk early. Hearing her mouth was the last thing he wanted to deal with while on vacation.

Murda sat back and watched Money as he attempted to sober up. He knew Money wouldn't be able to last after two more shots. Liquor wasn't his area. He needed to stick with smoking blunts all day. But then again, he still couldn't outdo him in that either.

"Yo son, you might as well call it quits. Over there looking like you about to throw up and shit. Need a bucket?" Murda picks up a napkin from the table and wipes Money's mouth as if he were a baby.

"Man, fuck you! This little bit of liquor ain't nothing. Yo bartender, let me get a double shot of Hennessey!"

"You over there sweating and shit like you're about to pass out. How you gon switch the game up and order some damn Hennessey. We're supposed to be drinking this foreign liquor," Murda said.

To the average eye, it looked like they were just getting drunk and having fun. They were celebrating their success of finding a new connect. A Jamaican cat by the name of Romario, who was moving weight and getting real money, his hands were involved in pretty much everything. From any type of automatic weapon, sex trafficking, coke, weed, heroin, pills. Anything you wanted or needed he could get if your money was right. Back in New York, the prices were super high and the quality of the coke was bad. It was so bad, a lot of their customers had either to turned to other dealers or had graduated to heavier drugs. Romario tried to explain to the young boys that the pills and heroin were the new thing. A lot of people didn't know that the pills such as Oxycontin and Percocet's contained the same ingredients as heroin causing people to become highly addicted.

Money and Murda didn't know much about the pill trade and wanted to stick with what they knew. A few times the coke they were getting had been switched with plain baking soda or Ketamine. They couldn't afford to keep taking losses. So, when they came across a connect who had pure, uncut cocaine for twenty grand. Immediately they jumped on the deal. The cocaine was so pure it shimmered like diamonds. Now all they had to do was take a trip to Miami to pick up the package and the deal would be complete. Life was about to get good for the two of them. But as the saying goes more money more problems.

"Well let's toast to a new connect, more money and my new bitch!" Money goes to put his glass in the air but stops as he catches on to the last of Murda's words.

"Whoa, my man what did you just say? New bitch? Don't tell me you've gone and wifed Sharnese's stuck-up ass."

"Watch ya mouth. I don't disrespect ya girl so don't disrespect mines." Murda tenses up a bit. He didn't mean to get so hostile about Sharnese. *Damn, this bitch got me tripping already and I haven't even fucked yet. Maybe this was a bad idea. I can't lose focus out here.* Throwing his head back, Murda takes another shot of rum to get his mind right. The burning sensation of the liquor makes it way down the back of his throat. Feeling relieved he apologizes to Money.

"My bad man, I didn't mean to come at you like that. Shawty got me tripping. I feel like she done put some type of voodoo on my ass. Got me even scared to fuck. I ain't never had a chick make me feel like this, and a young girl at that," Money didn't know what to say. In all his years of knowing Murda, he had never seen him like this over a girl. Sure, they'd both had their share of the neighborhood freaks, but seeing Murda wanting to be in a relationship was something new to them both.

Ever since Murda had his heart broken by his first love Tasha. She made it impossible for any female to get with him. Tasha had cheated on with one of his enemies. She informed him of everything she knew. From the stash house to when and where the drop offs would be made. Even down to every safe in his mother's house, providing them with the keys and security codes. It led to an all-out war between the two enemies. All because of a thirty-ass chick who wanted nothing but money. Tasha had blinded Money with good head and sex. He was caught slipping and a dick eating bitch was to blame. From that day forward, Murda vowed it was *Money over bitches* He hadn't had a relationship with a female since. Tasha had turned his heart cold. Meeting Sharnese made him feel like he could take that chance and love again. He knew it would take some time before he could completely trust her, but he was willing to give her a chance.

"Give her a try. I know it may seem too good to be true, but she's a good girl. Not like the thirsty chicks you see in the club always trying to get a dollar out of you. She really has a good head on her shoulders. Every nigga in the hood can't say they done been with her. Come to think of it, I never even heard her mention another nigga's name. So, just get ya mind right and make the best of it. We're supposed to be celebrating and you all in ya feelings and shit. Nigga man up and be prepared to get di money," Money always knew what words to say to bring his boy back around. Just as they were about to take another shot. Destiny and Sharnese took a seat at the bar.

"Here we are supposed to be exploring the island and you two fools are drunk already. Come on Money and get your drunk ass up so we can go check out our room and relax until later." Destiny smacks Money upside the head. She was pretty sure he would regurgitate at any minute, and she was not going to be the one to clean it up. Bending down so that she was his level she whispers in his ear.

Moving her hand into his lap she begins massaging his rod. Instantly, Money's tool stands at attention. He couldn't wait to slide inside her. Destiny's pussy stayed wet, whenever they fucked it felt like he was being recruited into the Navy. Not only was her sex game amazing, she should've been the next Super Head. She sucked his dick so good, she always left him speaking in tongues.

"Well, it looks like I'll be seeing you two lovebirds later. Wifey and I have some unfinished business to attend to."

Chapter Ten

"Shit, right there!" Those were the only words that Destiny managed to get out as Money held her legs high in the air putting her dick in her as far as it would go. *It should've been against the law for someone's dick to be so good.* Destiny thought to herself.

Hearing Destiny moan made Money pump harder. He made sure to hit all her spots. Being the freak she was, Destiny grabs one of her breasts and begins licking her nipples. With her free hand, she rubs her pierced clit, doing that sends her to cloud nine. Feeling himself about to cum, he pulls out of Destiny and turns her over on her stomach. Inch by inch, he eases inside of her. Instantly Destiny's juices spill over on his dick like a never-ending waterfall. Destiny bounces on his dick making sure to look at him while throwing her ass at him.

"Nigga, you better be catching this pussy while I'm throwing it," Money smacks her ass while pounding away.

"Damn, Des I'm about to cum." Money hollers out in complete ecstasy as he releases his seeds inside her. Laying back Money closes his eyes for a few seconds, not long after he was fast asleep. *Let me find out my shit so good it's putting niggas to sleep.*

Destiny couldn't help but laugh at the thoughts in her head. Not finished just yet, she climbs between his legs and licks the head of his dick. Lowering her body some more she places his dick in between her breasts and starts sucking the life out of him. Money opens his eyes and gets a good view. The feeling of her sucking away is like no other. With his hands behind his head, he moves his hips up and down trying to keep up with Destiny's rhythm.

One thing about Destiny she knew how to please her man, and didn't mind doing so. What one woman won't do another one will. They way Money took care of her he would be a fool not to be his personal freak. Anything that another bitch in the streets can do, she can do twice as good. She could even do some tricks on the pole. Money didn't know Destiny had been taking pole classes just to spice up things in the bedroom a little more. When it comes to her man she was willing to do anything in the bedroom except a threesome. Hell, he could even blindfold and tie her up but sharing the dick was nothing something she was willing to do. She might even let another bitch lick her clit, long as she didn't have to lick one back. But the dick was off limits, Destiny was stingy as hell. She wanted everything to herself.

Destiny takes him deep into her mouth until she feels it hit her tonsils. Spit drips from her mouth and she slurps every bit up. Up and down her head bobs, and without warning Money's thick, salty cum slides down her throat. If she wasn't a pro, she would've gagged. They both get up to take a shower where their sexcapade continues.

Chapter Eleven

Murda was supposed to have been enjoying the island with Sharnese, instead, he found himself wondering if the business was being taken care of like it should back home. He had left a young nigga in charge by the name of Pop. Without a doubt, Murda knew he would make sure his money was straight. It was Pop's temper that had him scared. It didn't take much to set him off. He had a no-nonsense policy. He was the type to shoot first and ask no questions. No matter how many times Murda tried to school him that every action didn't need a reaction, Pop just didn't comprehend, but none the less he was loyal. With the right guidance, he was bound to control an empire one day. He just had to learn how to relax. Murda liked for his team to move in silence. He loved for people to think he had fallen off. Only for him to come out of

nowhere and take over. If Rome wasn't built overnight, then how could they expect an empire to be?

"Yo Ma, you about ready to bounce?" Murda had something romantic planned for the two of them, but it was taking her a long ass time to get ready.

"Give me five more minutes bae," she yelled from out the bathroom.

"Typical women shit. They say five minutes, then five minutes turn into five hours," Murda said out loud.

Taking out his IPhone6 he sees twenty missed calls from Pop and all his messages were labeled urgent. Just as he was about to call Pop back his phone vibrates and a video message comes through. He recognizes the house in the picture as one of his trap houses, but it's been torn apart. Outside of the house stood four members of Kas crew. None of them bothered concealing their identity. Stepping forward in front of the camera is none other than Kaseem '*Kas'* himself. Murda nose flares in anger and his left eye begins to twitch. He sees red. Another message come through, this time things get real. The video had very little audio, but the message was loud and clear.

Jus, one of his workers was responsible for that house was bound to a chair. His hands were tied behind his back with rope and duct tape was secured over his mouth to keep him from making any sounds. One by one each man takes turns beating the man until he was conscious. Jus eyes swell up instantly, leaving him barely able to see. As if that wasn't enough, they dump cold water on him. Kas takes it upon himself to cut off each of his fingers, dropping them into a dog bowl. Murda stomach turns watching the blood squirt everywhere.

"I'm a murder, murder, murder, Murda!" Kas says as he circles around Jus pointing his gun at his temple. "Any last words ya bitch ass wants to say to ya boss."

"Fuck you!" Kas dumps all ten rounds into Justin's body.

"Murda, this ain't a game. I'm coming for you!"

Outraged, Murda grabs the vase from off the coffee table. Using all his force he throws the vase at the wall. Pieces of glass fly over the sitting area. Sharnese comes running out of the bathroom with her stun gun unsure of what's happening.

"Are you okay?" A concerned Sharnese asks. Still fuming with anger, Murda tries his best to regain his composure.

"Nah, I'm not alright. Some shit done popped off back home, and it needs to be handled asap. As much as I'd hate to cut this trip short, I'm a have to catch the first plane out in the morning. It's still early in the afternoon. We have plenty of time to enjoy each other's company."

Sharnese was a little disappointed that their time together would be cut short, but she was certain they would link up once they got back home. "It's fine. I can tell it must be something major. Considering the fact there's broken glass all over the floor."

"My fault, I ain't mean to scare you like that."

"Shit, I ain't know what the hell was going on. I thought we were getting robbed or some shit." Sharnese walks out on the balcony and admires the peaceful atmosphere. The sun was shining bright and the palm trees were blowing rapidly causing a nice breeze to blow. It was a perfect day to go water skiing. She wanted to try something she'd never done before. She had even thought about going swimming with the dolphins. Since the water was so transparent she had no fears about going under.

"That reminds me. Money mentioned he wants to speak with us about something at dinner. Not sure about what."

"Speaking of Money, I have to inform him of what went down."

The banging at the door startles them. The person on the other side of the door was covering the peephole. Using extra precaution, Murda grabs a butcher's knife from out the kitchen drawer. He could hear his heart beating inside of his head. Opening the door, he breathes a sigh of relief. It was nobody but Money playing.

"Whoa son, put that shit away. Who you trying to butcher up in here?" Money joked. Placing the knife down on the able, Murda leans up against the door.

"Man, some shit down went down back home. We'll talk about that later though. Right now, let's head on down to the restaurant."

"You sure bro? From the murderous look on ya face, I see that it's serious. If it's interfering with us getting this money, then we need to be on it now." *I don't know why this nigga talking in circles. If it's anything concerning my money I need to know now.*

I'll be damn if I'm risking my freedom for another muthafucka to fuck up mines. Shit, I got a wife and son to care for. I need every dime that belongs to me.

"Let's just discuss this after dinner. Yo Sharnese, let's go," Murda yells. Murda damn near loses his breath when Sharnese appears from around the corner rocking an all-white one-piece romper. The navy-blue wedges she had on her feet set the entire outfit. Her long Poetic Justice braids were wrapped in a tight bun on top of her head. This was the first time Murda really noticed her grey eyes. They helped bring out her facial features even more. Sharnese had natural beauty. Not one drop of makeup accustomed her face. The only type of cosmetic she applied was a coat of *Ruby Red* lipstick. Looking her up and down his eyes settled on the three-thousand-dollar Louie bag gripped tightly in her hand. This set off alarms in Murda's head.

I know she can't be making this much dough gluing a bunch of horse's hair into bitches heads all day He examined the bag thoroughly. It was no knockoff.

"Yo shawty remind me of what it is you do for a living again."

"Huh?"

"Huh, my ass. If you can huh you can hear. No offense, but every bag I've seen you with costs at least eight-hundred to a couple of thousand dollars. There are only two types of females that I know make that kind of money. Strippers and bitches who sell pussy for a living. I'm not judging you. Do you. At least let me know what I'm getting myself into." A smile plasters across Sharnese's face. She wasn't even mad at the accusations Murda had just mad. If she was him, she would think the same thing.

"No offense taken. My money is long and so is my clientele. I'm not new to this I'm true to this. I've been doing hair for years and I'm good at what I do. No scratch that. I'm the best at what I do," Sharnese says in confidence. "I supply my clients with grand A hair and top-notch service. Hell, if they want their hair to be laid like Beyoncé's then they need to pay life Beyoncé. Or else they can go buy some hair from the local beauty supply, look at tutorials on YouTube and fuck up their own heads. Anytime you see me step out it will be nothing but the best. The only thing fake I rock is weave and as you can see, I don't need that. Now that everything is cleared up I will be down in the lobby waiting for the two of you."

Sharnese struts past Murda making sure to put an extra switch in her walk. She was a boss bitch. If they both worked together, they were bound to become a power couple. The two were destined to become something great.

Chapter Twelve

To everyone's surprise, Money had reserved the entire restaurant for just the four of them. The tables were decorated in Destiny's favorite colors, pink and silver. The Chef had prepared a buffet-style dinner. Amongst the wall was a variety of Seafood. Snow crab legs, lobster tail, and jumbo shrimp. It also had some Jamaican jerk chicken with fried beans and rice. The dessert table consisted of all types of fresh fruit and rum cake. Destiny didn't know how to take it all in. Money always went out of his way to make sure she was happy, but this was something she wasn't expecting.

I wonder what he has up his sleeve. Everything is set up for some type of celebration. Our birthdays just passed and Valentine's day is still months away. You know what I'm a just sit back and enjoy the ride.

Just as everyone was getting comfortable Money goes and standing beside Destiny's chair. "Can I have everyone's attention, please? I know there's only the four of us here, but I would still like to thank you all for taking this last-minute trip with us." He turns to look at Destiny and starts pouring his heart out. "Des, you know I love you from the bottom of my heart. I know sometimes I'm not the easiest person in the world to get along with. You held a nigga down back when I was dirt broke and fucked up. You could've easily said fuck me and dipped off with the next nigga, but you stayed down. The love we share with each other is unconditional. Not only are you my ride or die, you're my better half."

Destiny's heart starts to beat fast. She could've sworn she saw a couple of tears drop from his eyes. She had never seen her man show this much emotion before. If she didn't know any better she would've thought he had some type of serious illness and that he was about to take his last breath. Money reaches into his pocket and gets down on one knee. *Oh my god! I know he's not about to do what I think he is.* Destiny's heart skips a beat and butterflies immediately flutter in her stomach. She grabs a glass of wine from off the table, swallowing it in one gulp. She waves the waitress over to pour another glass. She needed to prepare herself for whatever Money was about to say.

"On some real shit, you've been rocking with me for a minute now. When it comes to my son, you treat him just like he's your own. I'm tired of you playing wifey, I'm trying to make this here official. You down?" Reaching into his pocket, he pulls out a gold 24-karat gold diamond Princess cut engagement ring. Destiny jumps up and down.

"Yes, I'm ready to be your wife!" Tears of joy take control of her face. Destiny felt as if she was floating on top of the world. Popping a thousand pills couldn't compare to the high she was feeling. The last thing she expected Money to do was propose to her. Lately, he had been so occupied with handling business, they'd spent very little time together but that was the price you paid being involved with a street nigga.

"Everybody, drinks, and food are on me. Turn up!" Sharnese was overwhelmed with joy for her best friend. Destiny deserved it more than anything. She was the true definition of a rider. If her man had a problem in the streets, you best believe she was right there beside him. It didn't matter what the situation was. In her eyes, Money was always right. Even if he was dead, she was still riding with him. They were like Siamese twins, inseparable. Many females envied the relationship they had because Money had no problem saying he had a girl at home. Sharnese hoped to develop that type of relationship with Murda, even if it was too soon to tell where they would end up at.

"Congratulations, I'm so happy for you! I know you'll make a good wife. Hell, you're pretty much married now."

Thanks, girl! I still can't believe he asked me to marry him. Shit, I had to pinch myself to make sure I wasn't dreaming. Do you see this big ass rock he put on a bitch finger? My baby makes sure his girl wears nothing but the best!"

The diamonds on her ring glistened just like bright stars in a dark sky. For her not having a clue about the ring, Money had the size and style down pact. Anytime they went inside a jewelry store Destiny made it her business to check out the engagement rings. She just didn't know that he was paying attention. The D.J. turns on some music and plays Ki-Ci & JoJo's *All My Life* That song made the moment seem extra real. Money and Murda were enjoying the celebration until Money remembered something happened back home. Just that quick his business mode returned.

"Are you going to keep prolonging telling me what happened?" Murda jaws tighten. His facial expression is one of a cold killer. The look in his eyes was cold as he thought about the video he looked at earlier. Not able to talk, he pulls out his phone and hands it to Money. Just by seeing Kas, he became livid. He didn't need to see any more footage. He declared war. Money attempts to place the phone back in Murda's hand.

Murda shakes his head aggressively. "Nah, there's more."

Money could feel his heart sink to the bottom of his stomach. Without thinking he punches a hole in the wall. Blood covers his bruised knuckles. "I want all of them fucking dead immediately! I don't give a fuck if they're grocery shopping with their grandma. Those bitches have got to die!"

Money screamed at the top of his lungs frightening everyone around. Destiny races over to his side. All her years of being with him, she'd never seen him this upset. The man standing in front of her was unrecognizable. What she saw was a madman who had been possessed by a demon. She would never admit it, but she was scared.

"Bae, what's going on? What happened?" Destiny asks. With tears streaming down his face, Money grabs ahold of Destiny and places his head on her shoulder.

"They killed Jus. How am I supposed to explain this shit to his mom? How am I supposed to tell the mother of his unborn sot that he will never know his father?" Destiny knew this meant one thing. A war had just been declared.

"You can stay here for a few extra days if you want, but I'm catching the first plane out in the morning," Destiny didn't want to end her trip so soon, but when her man had problems in the streets so did she. Destiny ran the streets with Money. She had never come clean and told Sharnese. Destiny had put in more work than most niggas did their entire lifetime. She was a creeper. Staying low-gave her an advantage. The enemy never saw her coming.

"I guess there was a reason we never unpacked. Let's at least try to enjoy the rest of our night."

"Sharnese stood in the corner, staring out the window in deep thought. She was trying to digest all the events that had transpired over the night. Not only was her best friend getting married, but she had become the girlfriend of a savage. In her mind, she wondered if she made a good decision. From the way Murda reacted back in the room, she could tell he had a hot temper and it turned her on. Sharnese could feel her clit tingle and her nipples harden as she thought about the things Murda could possibly do in the bedroom. It had been a long time since she felt a man. Sharnese knew that once she was back home things would never be the same. Her good girl image was long gone. Murda was about to turn her world upside down.

Chapter Thirteen

Shoulders sideways, smack it, smack it in the air...

Legs moving side to side, smack it in the air...

Shoulders sideways, smack it, smack it in the air...

Legs moving side to side, smack it in the air...

Beyoncé's *7/11* blasted from the speakers as Brooklyn put on a show for her latest client. She had the entire hotel suite decorated in a romantic setting. There were vanilla scented candles lit everywhere, and red rose petals scattered across the floor. Since she was no longer dancing back in New York, she was now a full-time escort. Her funds had to come from somewhere. So, she figured why not get it the best way she knew how. Using what she has between her legs. During the day she sat in the hotel's casino scoping out potential clientele. Anybody she saw putting in more than a hundred dollars in the machine, she was on them. With money always being her focus, she had forgotten that someone was still out there trying to kill her.

The man she was servicing now was easy to please, but he had a sick fetish. He was an old racist white man named Kirk. While he hated black men, he loved the hell out of black women. He got off by calling her all types of black bitches while he sat back and jerked off. Kirk was seated in the corner of the room naked, except for the pink polka dot bowtie he had around his neck. Brooklyn wanted to ask him what was up with it, but she decided to leave it alone.

"That's it you black bitch, watch daddy cum!"

He moves his hand up and down in a fast motion. The man was so into his one- on- one session, he never noticed Brooklyn easing her hands into his pants pockets. She slowly turned around to make sure his eyes were still closed. Sure enough, he was still rubbing away on his little preemie dick. If he rubbed any harder the skin was sure to start peeling off. The sight of Kirk made her sick to her stomach. Kirk had to be every bit of seventy-years-old. He was so fat and sloppy, he had to use his free hand to hold up his sagging belly.

"Damn, I'm about to cum."

Brooklyn quickly snatches three hundred-dollar bills from out of his wallet. She tucks them under the mattress just as Kirk was busting off.

"Damn, I needed that," Kirk says while he's wiping the sticky cum from off his oversized stomach.

"Now you can get your ass up out of my room." Brooklyn pointed to the door. she was all about her money. She didn't have time for the small talk and she didn't want to know about his personal life unless it involved him giving up his social security number, bank accounts, and codes to his safe. Money did something to her that was unexplainable. It was like it gave her a high like no other. The highest grade of weed couldn't compare to the feeling she got when money came around her. Brooklyn just couldn't understand how so many females in the hood were always broke, yet gave up the pussy so freely.

Brooklyn was just about to go to the bathroom and freshen up when someone starts knocking at the door. *I know damn well this man ain't bring his ass back to my room. They know better to come to this room without having a scheduled appointment. He's not getting back in here unless he's trying to spend some of those Benjamin's.* Putting on her red silk robe, she opens the door but doesn't see anyone. *I know I'm not hearing shit, there was someone knocking at the door.* She walks down the hallway and she still doesn't see anyone.

Brooklyn felt like she was having Deja Vu. Taking her times, she makes her way back to her room. Stopping a few steps away from the door. Brooklyn's heart begins to race and she panics. In the doorway is yet another envelope, like the one that was left on her doorstep. Snatching up the envelope she runs into the room, slamming the door. *How the hell did this get here? No one was at the door or down the hall.* Brooklyn takes a deep breath. Using a box cutter, she opens the envelope. Inside is a piece of paper with the words: **YOU CAN RUN BUT YOU CAN'T HIDE BITCH** written in bold letters. Throwing on some regular street clothes, she grabs the duffel bag and makes a run for it. She looks around nervously as she constantly presses the down button on the elevator.

"I wish this fucking elevator would hurry up and open already," Brooklyn says to no one. A few seconds pass, and the door finally opens. She feels a sense of relief, but it doesn't last long. In the doorway of the elevator stands two Jamaican men that she'd seen before with Jean-Claude. Without thinking twice Brooklyn immediately turns around and makes a run for it to the stairs. By the time the Jamaican men realize what had happened, Brooklyn was long gone. Running down the street in traffic, Brooklyn is almost hit by a car. Panicking the driver exits his vehicle to make sure she's okay.

"Miss are you alright?" The concerned stranger asks. Brooklyn was stuck. Fear had taken over her entire body. All she could do was nod her head.

"No,"

"Is there somewhere I can take you?"

Brooklyn looks up the street and sees the two men coming. Snapping back to her senses she stands up. Barely in a whisper, she says “Those two Jamaican men coming up the street or trying to kill me. Please just gets me away from this area,” she pleads.

The unknown man looks up and sees the men. Slowly he helps Brooklyn inside his car while trying to get a good look at the men. He recognizes them as Bones and Cutter, the most ruthless members of the Shower Posse Crew. Getting in his Cadillac Elmira he pulls off. They ride in complete silence for twenty minutes.

“Yo Miss, do you have somewhere I can take you?” Lost in her own world, Brooklyn doesn’t hear a word the man says. Tapping on her shoulder, she jumps out of confusion.

“Brooklyn, my name is Brooklyn.”

“Well Miss Brooklyn, I’m Mark, do you have someone you can call or someplace I can take you?” Brooklyn had to admit it, but she really had no one she could call on. She had fucked over so many people, nobody wanted anything to do with her.

In a saddened tone, she replies. “No, I really don’t.”

Mark thinks long and hard about his next step. He didn’t even know Brooklyn but his instinct told him something about her wasn’t right. For the Shower Posse to be after her, she had to have crossed them in a major way. He didn’t know her or what her story was, but he was about to do some investigating about the mystery woman.

"I don't know what you're involved in but I would hate for something to happen to you. So, if you want I got an extra crib you can stay at out in Philly. You can stay as long as you need to get yourself together. I don't stay there much so you'll have the house to yourself."

Brooklyn looked at him like he was crazy and as her next possible victim. *Hmm, this nigga has got to have some money. He's driving a car that hasn't even been released to the public yet and he got Diamond Cartier frames covering his eyes. He's about to be my next victim and doesn't even know it.* Fake tears begin to roll down her face. "Thank you so much! You're an angel in disguise. I mean you know nothing about me and here you are willing to help a stranger. Another person would have easily tried to take advantage of a woman in my current situation. Please let me know if there's any way I can repay you."

Brooklyn didn't see the sinister smile Mark had on his face, it was a look that would have told her to jump out of the car. Moving and all. *Don't you worry your little face about repaying me? I'm more than certain there's a nice price on your head. Just as soon as I find out what you're involved in, I will be getting rewarded.*

"Not trying to be in your business or anything, but I'm gon need you to tell me what happened back there. Why did you have them two Jamaican men following you?" Brooklyn looked at him suspiciously. She was skeptical about if she could trust him with that type of information.

"How do I know you're not the police? Mark bit his tongue, to refrain from saying something slick out of his mouth.

"Don't ever say anything about the police to me ever again. I don't fuck with them pigs so go ahead and tell me what's up with the Jamaican cats that were chasing you," Mark had to calm himself down. Ever since he'd seen his mother and father gunned down by crooked cops, he was never fond of them. Normally, Brooklyn would have some slick comeback, but she remained quiet. That was the first time any man had made her freeze up,

"I'm sorry, I didn't mean to offend you. I just have a hard time trusting people," Brooklyn apologized.

The performance she was putting on was good enough to win her an Oscar award. Brooklyn was so good at manipulating people, she probably could have talked her way into Heaven. Brooklyn looks out the window and notices they weren't in the hood. All the houses they drove past had their front lawns mowed, and only foreign cars sat parked in the driveway.

"Are we in the right area? It doesn't look like black people live in this area."

Mark laughed. "Don't tell me you've never been out the hood before."

"A few times, nothing major. So, what type of work do you do?"

"Aren't you funny. You won't tell me what kind of trouble you're in, but you want me to reveal my profession. I'll think about telling you once you decide to spill the beans."

Brooklyn contemplates telling him. *What harm would it be if I told him? It's not like he could possibly know the people. Here we are way in Philly. I mean he seems harmless. But wait that's the same thing people say about me. What the hell, he might just turn out to be beneficial.*

Brooklyn decides against telling him the truth. She conjures up some bogus story about running away from an abusive ex-boyfriend that was trying to force her into the sex trade in Jamaica. Mark didn't believe one piece of the story she had just told. Yet, he went along with it anyway.

This bitch must think I'm stupid. Two big Shower Posse niggas are trying to kidnap her for her ex. Yeah right, she can tell that shit to someone else. There are a million bitches ready and willing to do shit like that and he just randomly wants to involve this girl. Shit ain't right. I'm hit my uncle up. He moves weight heavy for them. I'm sure he knows something about shawty.

The car slows down as they approach their location. Mark pulls up to a gated fence and enters a passcode. Brooklyn would have never thought he lived in this type of neighborhood. She blinked a few times, certain her eyes were playing a trick on her. The middle-class neighborhood was beautiful. Each house was at least two stories high. They had gigantic backyards, which consisted of full-sized swimming pools and hot tubs. Brooklyn could tell Mark lived amongst doctors and lawyers. It was really becoming obvious that Mark was getting money or knew someone who had plenty of it. Whatever the case was, she wanted parts of it.

Mark hit a few buttons on his phone, and the two-car garage open. Before backing in, he checks his surroundings. He was always careful about his safety. There was always someone around lurking, waiting for a quick come-up. Mark gives Brooklyn a tour of the house and shows her the room she'll be occupying.

"Are there any crazy baby mamas, stalking side chicks, or any thirsty thots that occasionally tend to pop up here?"

"Nah, You and I are the only ones that know about this place. I stay here when I need to get away. But the house is stocked with food, there's an extra car in the garage. I got business to handle so I'll be seeing you," Just like that Mark left the house.

Chapter Fourteen

It had been about two months since Sharnese had been in a relationship and thing were good on their end. Mama Peaches loved him, and he treated Sharnese like a queen. Now things in the streets had been crazy. Blood was being shed from both crews and bodies were dropping left and right. Murda had called a meeting with his entire squad. Product and money were coming up short and Kas was finding out information that he shouldn't have known about. There was a rat amongst the family, that had to be terminated for good. To Murda, being disloyal was the worst thing you could do. If you weren't loyal to the family then there was no way you could be trusted with money or anything else.

Everyone sat at the round table nervously. The area where the meeting was taken place would make someone think they were about to meet their maker. The abandoned warehouse gave off an eerie feeling. Even the hardest killers in the room felt like they would piss their pants. The secluded area did nothing to soothe their wondering minds. They had no idea why Murda had called a meeting with just about every member of the squad. The only time they all got together was to celebrate or make an example out of someone. Murda took a seat at the head of the table with Money.

"Today we are here to discuss a few ongoing issues. Product and money have been short or missing in out stash houses. At first, I thought it was a simple mistake. I figured a few of you forgot to report the money. That's not the problem. It's been occurring for the last three weeks and it's unacceptable. Each man that was in that house will be responsible for replacing the missing amount. Now if anyone begs to differ please speak now," Murda said to his entire congregation.

"Fuck this shit! I'm not about to pay for another nigga's fuck up. So yeah, I got a fucking problem with this!" Skeet says as he jumps to his feet.

"So, you really have a problem with these new orders?" Murda asks again making sure he's hearing right.

"I just said I did brah," Skeet said staring Murda dead in his face.

Murda smiles. Everyone knew that Murda smiling during any situation was dangerous for everyone. "Some of y'all seem to be forgetting who I am. Let me remind y'all," Pulling out his gun from his waist, Murda shoots Skeet in both in legs. Skeet never saw it coming as he dropped to the hard cement floor.

"Now is there anyone else who begs to differ?" No words left the mouths of the remaining men.

Murda releases the rest of the bullets into Skeet's body. It felt like his first time killing again. The adrenaline rush he got from shooting the gun had him wanting more. It was like an electrical shock had been sent through his body, making his dick hard. If he could've married the .45, he would've signed papers without thinking twice. A pool of blood begins to form from Skeet's body. With the snap of his fingers. The cleaning crew was there ready to dispose of the body and clean up any evidence.

"I hope that little demonstration made it clear to everyone that I'm not taking any more fuckups. Now that leads me to discuss the next topic. There is a snake lying in our grass. Someone in our family has broken the number one rule by associating with the enemy." The room goes so silent that if a feather was to hit the floor it could be heard. "Somehow they were tipped off about when we would be retaliating." Everybody looked at one another as if they were a suspect.

"No need for all that. The perpetrator has been seized. Pop would you please do the honor of bringing this nigga out."

Immediately Pop jumped up. It was his turn to prove that he was worthy of a promotion. He was tired of niggas sleeping on him. A lot of people underestimated Pop because of his small frame and that's where they made a big mistake. He may have been small but he had the strength of an ox and the wisdom of an old man. A lot of niggas lost their lives thinking they could run over top of him. Everyone's patience was thin as they waited for Pop to return. A few seconds later Pop comes back in escorted by two members of the cleaning crew and badly beaten Mikey. Mikey was so severely beaten his entire front teeth were missing. A knot the size of a golf ball stood out on his forehead. If you didn't know what he looked like before, then there was no way you would recognize him now.

Before Murda could finish his sentence, Pop went ahead and ended Mikey's life. His body shook violently as each bullet pierced through his flesh. You could count each bullet hole in his body. The white t-shirt he was wearing as now soaked in bright red blood. Pop had become disgusted from looking at the man who had placed Murda's life in danger. From this day on, he vowed to kill any man that thought they were going to take his mentor's life.

"You all have just witnessed what will happen to any of you when you decide to betray our family. Snitching will not be tolerated in any way. You may all leave now." Murda had to admit he was impressed with how Pop had taken control.

At home, Sharnese and Murda were celebrating their two-month anniversary. Murda mind begins to think about his father. *I need to go pay that man a visit. I know he's heard about this ongoing war with these bitch ass niggas. It's crazy how my father sold drugs and was a pimp back in the day and here I am following in his footsteps.*

"What's wrong baby? You know you can talk to me about anything," Murda drowned his sorrows in another shot of gin. He wasn't about to tell her about the war in the streets. He was constantly losing members and he wanted that nigga Kas dead!

"Nothing you would understand Ma, just some shit street niggas go through, that's all," Murda looks at Sharnese with pure lust. His eyes roam over every inch of her body. The effects of the alcohol were kicking in making him horny. Sharnese noticed the look in his eyes and decided it was about to go down. She leans forward and kisses him deeply in the mouth. Murda grabbed her waist and pulled her down into his lap. Since they had been lounging around in the house they were both already in a few pieces of clothes. She could feel how hard he was through his boxers.

Damn all this time I've been holding back, and this nigga is blessed between his legs. I knew better for this shit.

"Let's finish this in the bedroom."

Picking her up like a baby, Murda carries Sharnese into the bedroom. Placing her gently on the bed he reaches into the nightstand and pulls out a Magnum. After gently ripping open the condom he places it on his hard shaft. The sight of his dick sent chills down her spine. She knew it had to be at least ten inches long. Seeing the uncertain look in her eyes, he paused for a minute. He must have thought she was backing out. A quitter was something she wasn't. Sharnese was about to take the dick like a champ and throw her ass in all kinds of circles. Taking his time, he enters between her legs. She felt like she had taken a hit of the best dope you could find. Murda was gentle with every stroke he made. He took his time making sure that she felt him hit each one of her spots. He kissed her affectionately while he continued to pump in and out. When their bodies finally climaxed together, sleep took over them both.

Chapter Fifteen

The next morning Sharnese was woken up by the smell of breakfast. Climbing out of bed she walks into the bathroom and takes a quick shower. The smell of sex still lingered on her skin. Throwing on her personalized robe she joins Murda in the kitchen. She couldn't believe he was standing at the stove cooking.

"Good morning," she gave him a peck on his cheek.

"Morning Ma, I got some business to take care of today. So, you probably won't see me until later tonight," Murda says while stuffing a few pieces of bacon into his mouth.

"That's fine, I had planned on stopping by to see Mama Peaches today. It's been awhile."

"Alright ready to roll out. Come lock this door," Murda places his red fitted cap on his head, grabs his keys and heads out the door.

"Well look here. Today must be my lucky day. Let me give Kas a call and tell him the newly discovered information." Jermaine said out loud. Pulling out his phone, he places a call to his right-hand man.

"Sup cuz," Jermaine grinned into the phone.

"Shit, I can't call it."

"Well, I've got some shit that's gonna be music to ya ears," Jermaine had Kas's full attention immediately. "I see this nigga Murda coming out the building where I'm assuming he rests his head. I swear I want to end this nigga's life right here."

"Your fucking with me, right?" Kas had been trying to find out where Murda had been hiding. No one had seen him out in public. He had fallen off the face of the earth.

"Nah, I'm about to shoot you the address now," Jermaine watches Murda get in his car and pull off. Murda never even noticed the blue car that was parked across the street. Jermaine was about to end his call with Kas when Sharnese walks out the building to check the mail. "Hold up, his shawty just walked outside. Hold on for a sec while I snap a picture of this chick," Jermaine zooms in on his phone making sure to get a close view of Sharnese.

Kas mind went into overdrive. He was going to use Sharnese to his advantage. All niggas had a weakness and it was usually pussy. Kas started to put his plan in motion. He was about to prey on the weak.

"Good looking cuz, I owe you for this one. Go ahead and send that information to me. I'll get up with you later."

"No problem cuz," Jermaine shakes his head while pressing the end button. Sharnese had no clue what she had gotten herself into.

******

Sharnese was at Mama Peaches' house packing up the last of her things. She and Murda had finally decided to move in together. They had gone and rented out a nice house out in the Suburbs. Sharnese thought they had moved out there because Murda was making a lot more money. Murda just wanted her away from the streets.

"Have you heard anything from Brooklyn?" Mama Peaches asked. Sharnese thought long and hard. She hadn't spoken with her since the night of the fight which was strange. Normally, she would talk to Brooklyn at least once a day. She hadn't even been by to get her hair done but Brooklyn was known to do disappearing acts from time to time.

"Nope, I haven't talked to her in an about a month or so. I hope she's alright," Sharnese said while sitting down on the chocolate sectional.

"No news is good news. She must be doing just fine. I wouldn't be surprised if she done found a man with some money and is scheming on him. How is school coming along?"

"It's coming along great. I got a few more hours left before I'll be able to take my state exam," Usually it took a person at least nine months to complete school. Sharnese was so determined to open her own salon, the teacher made an exception and let her double her classes. With the help of Murda, she was able to purchase a nice sized shop in downtown New York. All she had to do now was get her business license and pass her state exam.

Sharnese began to reflect on everything her mother told her she would never be. Yet, she had managed to overcome every obstacle life had thrown her way. Any self-confidence she lacked before, she gained it all back. Murda made her feel like she was the most important woman in the world. Most men would have lost their interest once they realized no sex was involved. Murda had waited two months. She had counted down those days and to her their encounter last night was magnificent. He explored her body while connecting with her mind and soul. If the sex was going to be like that every night, she couldn't wait to move in the rest of her things.

Mama Peaches looked at Sharnese and smiled. She hadn't seen her this happy in a long time. She was aware of the extra activities in the streets that Murda had going on. She didn't approve of it, but she had to respect the fact he never brought it to her house. She knew his father Big Jimmy from her younger days so she couldn't blame him for the way he was. It was in his blood. Somethings you couldn't escape no matter how hard you tried. If it was in you, then it was in you. Trey Songz *Disrespectful* starts playing from Sharnese's phone. She looks at the screen and answers the call when she sees its Destiny. They hadn't talked in a few weeks. They had both been busy tending to the men in their lives.

"Hey girl, what's up?"

"Well, either somebody done finally gave up them drawers or you're just happy to hear from your best friend," Destiny laughed through the phone. No longer able to hold it in Sharnese feels her in on everything. "You've definitely said a mouthful. If you aren't busy can you hook my hair up? I would do it myself, but I don't have the patience to tackle this mess."

"You know I'm always available for you. What are you trying to get done?" Sharnese loved doing Destiny's hair. it always gave them time to gossip about whatever was going on in the hood.

"I was thinking about some Marley Twists. This weather has been humid as hell. I don't have time to be dealing with a weave in this heat."

"Okay, you got the hair?"

"Sure do."

"Good, I'll be there within the next hour or so. Make sure your hair is washed. I know how you get down and knowing you it's not washed," Destiny laughed. Sharnese knew her all too well. Sharnese hung up the phone and gathered her hair tools. "Alright Mama Peaches, I'm gone," Mama Peaches steps out the kitchen with an apron on and her hair tied. She didn't play about seeing hair in her kitchen.

"Alright baby, be sage and if you hear anything from your cousin give me a call. I hope you're going to get some of this food before you leave," she knew Sharnese was probably hungry so she had already fixed plates for her and Murda. The aroma of fried chicken, collard greens, homemade macaroni & cheese, and cornbread filled Sharnese's nose. Mama Peaches could cook her ass off. It was surprising to a lot of people that she hadn't opened her own restaurant.

"I'll be sure to give Murda his plate. That's if I don't get greedy and eat it all. Take it easy."

******

Destiny was just about to step outside and check the mail when she ran smack dead into Sharnese. "Girl, you can't be doing shit like that. I didn't even hear you pull up," All of a sudden Destiny felt dizzy. All the food she had eaten that morning found its way on the concrete sidewalk. Feeling slightly better she lifts her head up. Not even a minute later, she was throwing up once again. Sharnese sprays the food particles away with the water hose and then helps Destiny into the house.

"Hmm, is there something you're not telling me?"

Destiny had no idea what Sharnese was hinting at. Then it hit her. It had been awhile since she had her period. She thought maybe it had come from stress. There had been a lot going on in the streets with Money that had her worried. *I can't be pregnant! A baby is not something I want right now. There's a war going on and Money needs me. How the hell am I going to be able to defend my man with a big ass belly? These niggas won't respect me walking around pregnant. They gonna take me for a joke.* Tears roll down her face as the possibility of her being pregnant begins to sink in. She knew Money would be thrilled to be a father again. Deep down inside Destiny wanted to be someone's mother, but it was the fear that stopped her from being happy. She didn't want to raise her child into a lifestyle of drugs and violence. The thought of getting an abortion consumed her mind, but she knew Money would kill her if she even mentioned it. Quickly she erased the thought from her head.

"Being honest, I haven't had a period in about a month."

"Well don't you think it's about time for you to find out. You always keep pregnancy test underneath the bathroom sink. Go take one," Sharnese says as she taps her foot. "Here, get ya ass up and go piss on the stick." Destiny wasn't moving fast enough for her. Sharnese goes into the bathroom and gets it herself. "The sooner you do it, the sooner you'll feel better. Now go!" she shoves the pregnancy test inside Destiny's hand and gives her a gentle push.

"Okay Mother Sharnese, I'm going." Taking a deep breath Destiny reads the directions and pee on the stick. Those five minutes felt like an eternity. No longer able to refrain from peeking, she grabs the stick from off the sink and almost faints when she sees the two double lines. It was confirmed. A life was growing inside of her. She wasn't sure how she felt.

"Nese, come here quick!" Sharnese runs into the bathroom thinking something is wrong.

"It's positive!" Destiny whispered like a frightened little girl.

"Okay, call and make a doctor's appointment."

The next morning with Money by her side it was confirmed again. Destiny was indeed twelve weeks along. Seeing their growing baby on the ultrasound made every doubt she had exited her mind. Her and Money both agreed that she would stop running the streets with him so she could take care of her body. At first, it was a hard transition for her to get used to but with the extra time on her hands, she was able to pass her bar exam. Destiny was one step closer to opening her own law firm. It was one of her biggest accomplishments. Some people thought she was becoming a trader by being affiliated with the law, not realizing it would be helping them out in the long run.

Money and Murda sat in an old school box Chevy smoking a blunt. They had gotten a call about some unfamiliar faces walking around their territory. So far, they hadn't seen anything unusual, but to be on the safe side they were in the cut checking things out.

"This some good shit, brah. Where you find this at?"

"Some young niggas around the way was pulling they ass about having the best so you know I had to try it out myself." Murda passed the blunt back to Money. He only smoked enough to relax his mind. He couldn't afford to be caught slipping by Kas and his crew again. Money looked out his back window and noticed an all blue Impala creeping up the street. Grabbing his gun from under the front seat, he taps Money.

"Looks like dem niggas want problems today," Murda and Money both cock their gun's back and start blasting off.

One of the bullets hit the driver causing the car to spin out of control. Smoke emerges from the car. Within seconds it went up in flames. Murda and Money were satisfied with the fact that they had blown up and entire car with niggas from Kas's crew. Sirens could be heard in the background. They knew they had to get out of dodge before they were taken downtown. News spread quickly to Kas. That night a deadly massacre occurred, anyone associated with Murda's crew was killed. Churches were shot up and innocent children were killed all because Kas had a point to prove.

Chapter Sixteen

It had been a few weeks since the deadly attacks. The police force was out swarming the streets left and right. You couldn't even walk down the street without them pulling you over to check for warrants. A lot of people who had nothing to do with the war were getting thrown into police cars. With both crews steady losing members, they were forced to lay low for a while. Murda no longer wanted to involve innocent people in their beef. It was now personal for him. he wanted Kas dead for his own reasons.

Murda and Sharnese had decided to grab a bite to eat at Sylvia's. Sylvia's was one of the best soul food restaurants in Harlem. Any given day you were liable to run across celebrities visiting to get a taste of their fried chicken and baked macaroni and cheese. They both take a seat at a booth in the corner of the restaurant. It was a routine Murda had developed. He never sat with his back facing anyone. He needed to be able to see everything at all times. The waitress walks over ready to take their orders.

"Hi my name is Monica and I'll be your waitress tonight. Are you ready to order?" the waitress pulls her pen and notepad out of her apron pocket. It was a Friday night and she was beyond tired. The restaurant was only going to get busier once the clubs let out.

"Yeah, let me get the chicken and waffles with an iced tea."

"And for you Miss?"

"I'll take the fried catfish with potato salad and collard greens, and I'll have a Bloody Mary to drink," The waitress grabs the menu and goes to tend to their order. The two lovebirds engage in small talk about things going on in the news. A Malaysian airplane carrying two hundred and thirty-nine people had just up and vanished into thin air.

"I'm telling you all this shit was stage by the government. How in the hell do you just lose a plane full of people? You lose house keys, credit cards and shit like that. I wouldn't be surprised if they got them at a secret location experimenting on them," you couldn't tell Murda he didn't know what he was talking about.

Sharnese had never thought about those theories before, but they were quite believable. The two were so engaged in their conversation they never noticed that a brown-skinned girl with platinum blonde hair had approached their table.

"Cortez De'Mario Rodriguez! Is this the bitch that got ya mind fucked up that you can't return my damn phone calls," a pissed off Chanel screamed at the top of her lungs, causing unwanted attention from the other customers.

"Oh shit!" Murda said out loud a she looked up. Chanel was a freak bitch he fucked around with a few times when he and Sharnese had first got together. It was nothing serious between the two. She was just someone he would call on whenever he needed to bust a nut. Murda cut her off when she started asking for money in return for her services. He wasn't about to pay for something he could get from anywhere. Especially when her pussy wasn't even good.

"Murda, what the hell is going on?" a confused Sharnese asked. "And who the hell are you calling a bitch?"

"I'm calling you a bitch, bitch!" Chanel loved the commotion she was currently creating. She had heard around the hood that Murda had gotten a new bitch and was treating her like a queen. So yeah, she wanted to see what all the hype was about.

"Ya ass got some explaining to do and now! What the fuck is this bitch talking about?" Sharnese yells.

"Come on Ma, let's just go. We don't need all these extra people in our business," Murda was embarrassed that a situation like this was even happening. Chanel knew better than to try some shit like this. He wasn't some regular nigga. He runs the fucking streets. He would blow a nigga's head off for looking at his girl the wrong way, and here some thot had the nerve to be disrespectful in a public place.

"Yes, please explain to your bitch about us," Chanel rubs her big belly with a wicked smile on her face. This was the first time either of them noticed that she was carrying a baby.

I know this bitch is crazy now. Ain't no way in hell that baby she's carrying mines. I made sure I wrapped up every time, or at least I think I did.

"Bitch, that baby ain't mines."

"Did you fuck her?" Sharnese asked with tears beginning to form in her eyes. The thought of being cheated on crushed her soul. In her eyes, he was the perfect man, and nobody could tell her anything different. But she wasn't about to sit around and play nobody's fool either. As far as she was concerned their relationship was officially over until she found out if that was his baby. Seeing that Murda had very little to say about the situation told her everything she needed to know. Sharnese picks up her drink and throws it in his face. "Fuck you, we're done! Lose my damn number.

And for you bitch, I'll definitely be seeing ya ass after you drop that load."

Sharnese rushes out the restaurant, not sure where she was going since she didn't drive her own car. One thing she did know was that it was getting too late to be walking the streets alone. For a minute she thought about calling Destiny but didn't want to bother her. Besides she knew once she told her what had happened she would be ready to shoot up the entire place and calling Mama Peaches was out of the question. It was a Friday night and she was probably out on a date. Thoughts of Murda cheating on her started to replay in her mind. She couldn't believe that the man she put all her trust in had betrayed her in the worst way.

Kas had been parked across the street the entire time, watching everything unfold. He couldn't believe that his plan was coming together so effortlessly. He paid Chanel a few stacks to start some drama between Murda and Sharnese, not knowing Chanel and Murda had unfinished business. Kas continued to follow Sharnese for a few more blocks before finally deciding to pull up beside her.

"Excuse me, Miss," he slowed down the car and Sharnese jumped at the sound of the unfamiliar man. She was so consumed with her own thoughts that she never heard the car creep up on her. Unaware of what the man wants, she picks up her and pace and continues to walk faster.

"Yo, you need a ride or something? A lady shouldn't be walking the streets this late by herself," she stops in her tracks and takes a minute to analyze her current situation. She had no transportation and taking the subway was out of the question. Going against her better judgment, she slowly walks towards the car. The handsome man behind the wheel didn't look a bit harmful. "

"Get in. I'm Kasseem, but you can call me Kas for short," Kas unlocks the door and Sharnese gets in.

"Sharnese," she says. As she climbs into the car she grabs hold of her purse extra tight. Sharnese didn't care how good Kas looked. If he tried anything stupid she was going to tase him with her stun gun.

"Is everything alright? Where are you headed?" he asked.

That's' when it dawned on her that she wasn't sure where she was going. She just knew she wasn't going back to the home that he shared with Murda. Reluctantly she had no choice but to give him Mama Peaches' address. As if she wasn't already feeling down, Donnell Jones *Where I Wanna Be* plays from the car's speakers. Sharnese falls into a deep depression. She couldn't stop the tears that managed to fall down her face. Her heart felt like it had been torn into a million pieces.

"Here," Kas hands her some tissues to wipe her face. Her once flawless face was now smeared with black eyeliner. "You want to talk about it?" Kas asked her. He really didn't give a damn what her problem was, but she had been crying loud as hell since he picked her up. Thank God, they didn't have too far to go. He didn't know how much more of the crying he could take. Sharnese takes a deep breath as she relives the events that had just taken place.

"I just found out that my boyfriend…well my ex-boyfriend cheated on me and possibly even have a baby on the way."

Saying those words made the pain hurt even more. She just couldn't accept the fact that Murda had cheated on her. She was no different from any other female. She really thought they shared something special.

"Typical nigga shit."

"What do you mean by that?"

"A nigga gon be a nigga, simple as that. Every day bitches get cheated on. It doesn't matter how good you look, how fat ya ass is, or if you make ya own money. If a nigga gon fuck another bitch, that's just what he gon do." For some reason, Kas felt like she needed a lesson on how niggas get down. She seemed lost as hell.

"Since it's typical nigga shit, I just bet you cheat on ya girl all the time huh?" Sharnese was suddenly regretting the entire conversation. As she looked out the window she notices she's just five minutes away from Mama Peaches' house.

"See, that's where you're wrong. Haven't you ever heard of the saying a person who assumes usually ends of making an ass out of themselves? I have no girl," Kas smirks. He knew he had hit her with something to think about for a minute.

"I didn't mean to offend you."

"You didn't," an awkward silence filled the air as the car comes to a stop. Sharnese was surprised to see that Mama Peaches was still up. For a few minutes, she sat in the car trying to get herself together. She knew Mama Peaches would have a thousand questions as to why she was there.

It's either now or never. Ain't no way this girl getting out this car without giving me her number. I'm tired of playing games with Murda's ass. I want him dead!

"I know this is a fucked-up time to be asking, but would you like to grab a bite to eat sometime?" he figured Sharnese probably thought he was crazy for asking her when they had just met, but he didn't care.

"Um sure, I suppose." Her mind was playing tricks on her. One part of her was screaming tell this strange man hell no! While the other part was telling her to give Kas her number so she could take her mind off Murda. They both exchange numbers and say their goodbyes. Before she's able to step foot in the door Mama Peaches is standing there waiting for her. She had been looking out the window the entire time.

"What brings you by this time of night, and who was that boy?"

"If you must know, he name is Kaseem and he just happened to give me a ride here," she sighed.

"Okay, where is Murda and why couldn't he give you a ride? You've yet to explain what you're doing at my house this time of night. If I'm not mistaken you live on the other side of town."

This woman is determined to make my night worse than what it has already been. All I want to do is take a hot shower and curl up in bed. Is that too much to ask for? Damn! Sharnese knew better than to say what she was thinking out loud.

"Mama Peaches, can we not talk about him? I've had a long night and I just want some sleep," Sharnese could hear her voice trying to crack. She was trying her hardest not to shed another tear over that man, but it was becoming extremely difficult. Her emotions were getting the best of her. Murda steady blowing her phone up didn't make the matter much better. She planned on talking to him eventually, just not right now.

Mama Peaches could see that Sharnese was upset so she decided to end the conversation, for now. Whether Sharnese wanted to or not she was going to tell her what happened, even though she had a pretty good idea what was wrong. You could tell a man about the consequences of playing with a woman's heart and they still chose to do it. Some of them failed to realize that one day they would have daughters. The same way they were hurting someone's daughter, some boy will hurt their daughter's too. Mama Peaches had been cheated on one too many times in her day. She knew the signs of a broken heart all too well so she let Sharnese go on about her business.

Chapter Seventeen

Brooklyn had been staying at Mark's house for quite some time now. It felt good not to be looking over her shoulder for a change, but Mark was very different. No matter how often she walked around the house in just a thong, ass jiggling everywhere, he never once tried to sleep with her. If she didn't know any better she would swear he was gay. Mark was a man of very few words. Whenever he did stop by, he was always downstairs in his study room. Brooklyn had never been inside, but from the little, she did see it reminded her of a huge library. There were books everywhere and all the furniture was Cherry Wood. Mark was secretive about the room. she wasn't sure what he had hidden in there, but she was determined to find out. Plus, she couldn't live off her stash forever. She was going to search his house high and low until she found some dough.

Brooklyn was just about to make her way down to the study when she heard the door open. Quickly she runs inside of her room. Trying not to make any noise she listens quietly to Mark while he's on the phone. From what she could make out of it, he was making some arrangements.

"I hear everything your saying. You just make sure you have that thing ready for me," Brooklyn had heard enough. To her, it sounded like Mark had a date. She just hoped it wasn't with a man. When she could no longer hear him talking on the phone she assumed he went down into his study. Out of nowhere a strong hunger pain shot through her stomach. Any plans of snooping around were now on hold until she got something to eat. She could taste Shrimp Tacos on the tip of her tongue. Being so used to eating out all the time, being in a kitchen felt foreign to Brooklyn.

"You got it smelling good in here, just don't burn my house down," Mark smiled showing off his perfect pearly whites.

"Thank you," *I can't believe this nigga is really speaking to me.* It fucked her head up to hear Mark saying more than two words.

"I didn't know you could cook," he said as he sampled pieces of the Shrimp Tacos. Licking her lips seductively, she picks up a piece of shrimp and slowly sucks the juices off.

"That's not all I can do either," *this nigga can front all he wants, but the bulge in his pants in telling me everything I need to know.* Brooklyn was determined to get the dick even if it meant she had to take it. Her hormones were in overdrive. It had been a minute since she had felt a man inside of her.

I don't know why this girl insists on trying to throw her pussy at me. It's not like I haven't noticed how fat her ass was in that thong the other day. I've just had other things on my mind but god damn the way she sucked that shrimp got me reconsidering, I wonder what her mouth feels like.

Without warning, Mark dropped his pants right there in the kitchen and walked into the living room. He wasn't about to waste any time getting straight to it.

"Are we fucking or what? Don't just stand there with ya mouth open. Come show me what you all about," Mark was tired of playing mind games with Brooklyn. She had been acting like she was pressed for the dick for some time. Niggas only did the type of shit she had been doing. He had never been around a female that wanted the dick so badly. He couldn't lie, it turned him on.

Mark just didn't know Brooklyn was about to give him the thrill of his life. Not only was she about to fuck his brains out, but the way she was about to suck his dick was guaranteed to make him hers. Her head game was wicked. Brooklyn pushed Mark down onto the loveseat sofa. She wasted no time pulling his pants and boxers down to his ankles. Her mouth hung low in astonishment. She couldn't believe he was working with such a huge package. Greedily she takes all ten inches in her mouth and goes to work.

"Ahh," Mark screamed out in excitement as his body twists and turns. The pleasure he was receiving made his eyes roll to the back of his head and his toes curl. His body begins to convulse as he's about to reach his peak.

His ass is crazy if he thinks he's about to but already. I haven't even had a chance to ride the dick yet, and here this nigga is about to tap out. She didn't give him a warning when she jumped on top of him and begin riding him like a cowgirl. Shit for a minute she thought she was in her own personal rodeo. With their bodies enclosed together, Mark palmed her ass and pumped up and down. Before they knew it, they were both breathing hard, barely able to breathe. Mark's sex game left Brooklyn speechless. She thought she was about to fuck him and ended up getting fucked!

"You sure you ain't some undercover porn star?" Mark had to ask. The way Brooklyn had just sucked his dick wasn't normal. Her nickname should've been vacuum lips. He was surprised he still had skin left as hard as she was sucking.

Brooklyn laughed, "Nah, I'm just an expertise in the bedroom that's all."

It was sad she wouldn't be around much longer. Mark would not have minded keeping Brooklyn for his own personal sex slave. Marl goes into the bathroom and washes up. While he's in there his phone rings. When he exits the bathroom, he's in a rush. "Sorry I have to leave so soon, but I got some business to take care of."

"No problem, I got what I wanted anyway," Brooklyn winks her eye and smiles.

Brooklyn scrambles to find her clothes that were scattered throughout the kitchen and living room. Taking a shower was the last thing on her mind. She wanted to find out what Mark had in his office. She peeks out the blinds to make sure he's gone. Sure enough, she could see him speeding down the street. Making her way downstairs she stops. *This man has been nothing but good to me and here I am about to go looking for a stash. Oh well,* lightly she turns the knob on the door. Surprisingly it's unlocked. The first place she checks in his desk. One by one she opens each of the drawers and finds nothing. Growing frustrated she slams the drawers shut.

"Where the fuck is the cash at?" she screams out loud.

Just then her eyes zoom in on a black file cabinet in the corner. When she opens the top cabinet a tan folder with her name on it catches her attention. Flipping open the folder there are pictures of her back in New York. Going through more photos she comes across some men who appear to be of Jamaican descent. Looking closer, one of them happens to be the man she killed at her house. *What the fuck is really going on? Was Mark following me the entire time? Or was this a setup?* Money was no longer on her mind.

Mark knew it was only a matter of time before Brooklyn's money hungry ass went lurking around the house. Brooklyn was so clumsy she didn't notice the surveillance system throughout the entire place. Mark pours his concoction of Chloroform onto a white cloth napkin. He knew Brooklyn would put up a good fight if he tried to kidnap her so this is the only way it would work. There was no he was going to get away. She had a nice price on her head. After doing some investigation of how own. Mark had found out she had stolen money from his uncle, and he wanted her dead or alive. With his back against the wall, Mark waits until she comes out the study. Just as she's about to close the door he makes his move.

Out of nowhere, Brooklyn feels a pair of hands grab her from behind. Trying her hardest to get a glimpse of the intruder, she recognizes Mark's long dread. She couldn't understand what was happening. She uses all the strength she has and elbows him in the ribs. It was pointless. Mark didn't even flinch.

"What do you want with me?" Brooklyn asked. That was a wrong move. When she goes to speak again Mark places a piece of cloth over her mouth. She didn't know what was inside the cloth, but she felt herself losing consciousness. Brooklyn starts to feel lightheaded and before she can begin to process what's happening, everything around her goes black. After making sure the coast is clear Mark proceeds to put Brooklyn's body in the trunk of his car. Mark had completed his end of the deal. It was time for his uncle to pay up. What he did with Brooklyn wasn’t his business. As ruthless as he was he could only imagine what he has in store for her.

Chapter Eighteen

It has been weeks since Murda had heard from Sharnese. He had been blowing up her phone non-stop. No matter how many times he tried calling she just wouldn't answer the phone. Murda had sent flowers, bears, and types of gifts to Mama Peaches house, just to have them all sent back. He hated that he fucked up what they had. Sharnese had him feeling love-sick. Then on top of that, there was still the bullshit with Chanel. Murda hadn't fucked with Chanel in months, and suddenly, she pops up pregnant, talking about the baby is his. He didn't want to admit to no one that he'd gone inside Chanel raw a few times, but he always made sure he pulled out.

Chanel's freaky ass was always after some nigga's dough. She was nothing more than a thirsty Thursday hoe. You know the type that was trained to go. She'd do anything for the dick if the price was right. There was no telling who all could've possibly gotten her pregnant. Until a DNA test was performed, Murda was not claiming her baby. He wasn't about to be her meal ticket out the hood. Chanel better ++be prepared to get all the assistance from the state that she could. One day he wanted to be a father but not under these circumstances. Times like this there was only one person who could give him good advice. Murda hops in his car and heads over to pay his father a visit.

Cruising up the lane Murda couldn't help but admire his father's mansion. In the very middle of the circular driveway stood a marble fountain with the letter J. On anything he owned it was mandatory that his initials were engraved on it. The mansion had eight bedrooms, six full baths, a huge library and full gym loaded with exercise equipment. The entire flooring had marble tiles encrusted with diamonds and pearls. Every room was furnished with Italian furniture and expensive Italian artwork to accompany it. One-day Murda planned on being boss status just like his father. The amount of money he had now was nothing compared to what his father had acquired back in his day. The only difference now was all his illegal money was clean. Not a penny could be traced back to drug money.

When he rang the doorbell, he was greeted by his mother. No matter how many years went by, she didn't seem to age. The glow she wore on her face let him know life was treating her good. "Hola mama," he says as he pulls her in for a huge bear hug.

"Hola el bebe. Su padre es la parte de atras."

"Gracias mama," although his mother was a full-blooded African-American, she had been around his father so long she mainly spoke Spanish. One could not look at her and tell she was black. Her long black hair and high yellow skin gave her the appearance of someone who was mixed. Back by the lake was his father. The one and only Big Jimmy.

Jimmy was always aware of his surroundings, he heard Murda coming before he even approached him. He looks at his son and continues to take a puff from his Cuban cigar. Clouds of smoke form in the air. From the way, he was dressed you would have thought he was still a pimp. His long jet-black hair which was slicked back into a ponytail and his gigantic gold pinky ring did nothing to make you believe otherwise. He was most definitely a boss. Whenever he stepped into a room his presence demanded respect.

"Son have a seat," he reaches into the cooler and hands Murda a beer. Murda takes it and chugs his down in a few seconds. Big Jimmy hands him another one.

"What's on your mind? You over there looking like you just lost your best friend."

Damn is it really that obvious? I haven't even been here ten minutes and already he can tell something isn't right. I really need to get my shit together. If he can see it, there's no telling what everyone else can see.

"Man Pops, I done messed up," he takes another sip from his beer. The taste was disgusting but refreshing at the same time. He'd rather have liquor any day.

"Let me guess, woman problems?"

"More like women problems," Murda tells his father about the drama he's gotten himself into. Murda feels like a woman gossiping in the beauty salon. Big Jimmy's facial expression change a couple of times as Murda continues with his story. One thing about Big Jimmy was you could never tell exactly what he's thinking. He could have the biggest smile on his face and be ready to kill you any second.

As he sits and listens to Murda tell his story, he starts to reminisce about his younger days. Back when he and Carmen decided to make things official he still had one hoe in the stable that he messed around with from time to time named Diana.

Twenty-seven years earlier....

"Bitch, you must be asking to visit ya grave early! I don't give a rat's ass about what you and Jimmy were doing before I came along. I'm here now and your ass will respect me or you will go," Carmen screamed making sure not only Diana heard her but every other girl in the house. She didn't understand why Diana thought because she was young and petite that she wouldn't fuck her up. Out of all the girls, Diana was the only one who kept trying her. She just didn't know Carmen wouldn't hesitate to go upside her head with one of the iron skillets in the kitchen. The easy way or the hard way Diana was going to learn to respect her!

Crazy thoughts ran through Diana's head as she was fighting with Carmen. There was no way in hell she was going to let some young piss hopper come in and take her place. Before Carmen came along she was Jimmy's bottom bitch. Anything he asked her to do,, she would do it. Hell, all he had to do was tell her how high to jump and you damn right she was gonna do it. Every day Carmen walked around like she was hot shit. Like she was better than her because he had taken her off the stroll. Diana couldn't believe that Jimmy had fallen in love with Carmen. All these years she'd been cooking his meals, washing his dirty drawers and sucking his dick on call and he still chose another bitch over her. On several late-night occasions after one of their bomb sex sessions, he whispered in her ear about how he wanted to marry her one day. Like a dumb ass, she believed him. There was never a time he had to question her loyalty to him. So why he didn't choose her, she just didn't understand. Her many of questions sent her mind into overdrive. She didn't know what to think.

"I don't care about none of that shit you are popping out ya mouth. You might not be putting in no work, but look around boo you're still living in the same house as the rest of us hoes. All you need to know is every chance I get I will be spreading these legs for Jimmy."

Every word she spoke out of her mouth she meant. The only way she would ever stop fucking Jimmy was if he told her it was over himself. Carmen had another thing coming if she thought

Diana gave a damn about her feelings. Why should she? A bitch never gave a damn about hers. No one could imagine the evil thoughts that were going through her head. She badly wanted to grab a knife and slice her throat. She knew for sure Jimmy would kill her if she did. They both must've thought she didn't know about the little bastard child they were having. She'd spotted the pregnancy test in the bathroom trash one morning. It fine with her though, she had a nice trick up her sleeve for the both of their asses. They weren't the only ones hiding things.

Every month Big Jimmy always sent a doctor in to test the girls for STD's and to ensure they were all on birth control. Diana had slipped the doctor a couple hundred not to give her the Depo shit. Shit, if the only way she could grab his full attention was to trap him with a baby then so be it. She had no problem doing it. If she couldn't have him all to herself then they both will be having a child that shares the same both as Jimmy. Never in a million years did she imagine she would have been so desperate for love…well not for just anyone's love but Big Jimmy's love. The more time he spent with Carmen, the more she felt herself turning into some kind of a psychotic bitch. She was constantly stalking his every move. Big Jimmy was outside busting a few licks when he heard a bunch of yelling coming from inside the house.

"Why must these two bitches go at each other's throats every damn day," Big Jimmy says out loud to himself. He goes inside to see what the hell is going on. The screaming and

yelling were so loud it could be heard down the street. "I really got to do something about this before one of our nosy ass neighbors decides to call the police. Don't these bitches know I'm dirty as hell? The last thing I need is for my money to be messed up over some dumb shit." Jimmy walks into the house pissed off. Diana and Carmen ignore his presence and continues to go back and forth. "What the fuck is the problem in here?" Both women freeze in place. The sound of Big Jimmy's silenced the room. "Oh, so you two are deaf now huh?"

"Babe, I'm sick of this bitch thinking she can do and say what she wants. None of the other girls give me a problem except her," Carmen whined in her best baby voice.

"Diana, you are going to have to start respecting Carmen. Things are different this time around now that she's next to be in charge." Diana couldn't believe her eyes.

"This young bitch is really taking my place?" she says to no one. Diana sees red and wants revenge in the worst way. What better way to get it other than to reveal her secret? "Well Jimmy, I have something that I need to talk to you about in private." Carmen rolled her eyes. Diana was starting to get on her last nerve.

"No, anything that you have to say to my man you will say in front of me also."

"Perfect!" Carmen was making things a lot easier for her. "Sure, if you insist," Diana could feel little butterflies

fluttering in her stomach. She couldn't tell if she was about to get sick or what as nervousness took over her entire body. The tough girl role that she had been playing was no longer there. She wasn't quite sure how this scenario was about to play out.

"Well um," Diana takes a moment to gather her words together. Saying something that was so easy was taking her forever. All the mouth she had and she was having a hard time to Jimmy what she had to say. "I'm pregnant," there it was; she had finally gotten it out. The look on Carmen's face was one Diana would never forget. She looked as if she was about to pass out. Big Jimmy's face, on the other hand, held a blank expression. She wasn't sure if he was excited or mad as hell.

"You bitch, you set me up! I pay good money every month to have a doctor make sure y'all are protected against this kind of shit. You will get rid of that baby as soon as possible!" Diana's heart was crushed. Those were the last words she expected to hear him say. If anything, she thought he was going to say that they were about to start a family, but she was wrong.

"I'm not getting rid of our child."

"Oh no, don't you even try that. Either you get an abortion or get the hell out!"

"No Jimmy, she doesn't have a choice. Her ass has to go, now!" To say Diana was hurt would have been an understatement. Carmen wanted to slap the hell out of her ass but

there was no way she was gonna give Diana what she wanted. As much as she wanted to give Jimmy the benefit of the doubt. She knew Diana wasn't lying about the two of them still fucking around. This was the last time he was going to make a full out of her.

Inside the bedroom, Carmen kept her Desert Eagle hidden for purposes like this. She knew the day would come when she would have to prove herself. For a moment, Carmen had forgotten all about the unborn child she was carrying. Her mind had blacked out and she was in another world. She closes her eyes and starts pulling the trigger.

Moving her hands from left to right, she doesn't care that her aim was off as long as she hit someone. "Damn it, you crazy bitch you shot me!" Big Jimmy hollers through clenched teeth.

Carmen opens her eyes to see if she had done any real damage. Jimmy's pants leg was soaked in blood. She figured she must have shot him in the leg. It was funny as hell seeing Jimmy on the floor crying like a baby in pain. Mr. Untouchable had finally been touched. Instead of feeling remorseful for what she had just done, she smiles. Walking over to Jimmy she grabs hold of both his jaws extra tight and squeezes them until she can't anymore.

"Next time I promise I won't miss. Let this be my first and last warning."

All Jimmy had come into the house for was to stop Carmen and Diana from killing each other and he ended up getting shot. He didn't even know Carmen had a gun, let alone knew how to shoot one. How was he supposed to know that Diana was going to drop that kind of bomb on him? But like all things, what's done in the dark always come to light. He just wasn't expecting it to come out this way. He could understand Diana's reasoning for being hurt. She was the very first girl on his team. Truth be told he could never see himself with her exclusively. Too many Johns had run through her and she was no longer in her prime. You can't teach an old dog new tricks. But with Carmen, she was young and naïve. All Jimmy had to do was dick her down good and she would obey. They both were so busy staring each other down they never noticed Diana had slipped out the door. That was the last time Jimmy heard anything from her.

Present day…

"Son, in this situation the best thing for you to do is man up. Let her have her space. It's gonna take some time before she forgives you, but eventually, she will. Things between your mother and I haven't always been peaches and cream," Jimmy rolled up his pants leg and shows Murda his gunshot wound. "Believe it or not, your mother once shot me for my cheating ways."

The look on Murda's face was remarkable. His mouth hung low as he examined the scar the bullet left. "Nah Pops, I don't believe Mom Dukes did no shit like that," *Damn, let me find out Mom Dukes was busting that gun back in the day* the image that lingered in his head was a funny one. Carmen shooting Big Jimmy, now that's something you paid money to see.

"Son, you've got a lot to learn about women. Your mother is not as innocent as you may think. If you don't remember anything else, remember this. A woman scorned is a very dangerous woman. When a woman's fed up there's no telling what she'll do to seek revenge. Trust me, I've lived it."

"Yeah Pops, you're right. I understand where you're coming from. Enough with the love talk thought, I'm ready to discuss business. Just thinking about the ongoing beef with Kas made his blood boil. Murda had been trying to track him down for weeks and still hadn't been able to retrieve any information on his whereabouts. Murda's patience was running thin. He wanted this nigga dead like yesterday. He wouldn't be able to sleep at night until he knew for sure Kas was six feet under.

"How's everything look out there?"

"To be honest, everything's been moving so fast it's scary. It's like no matter how much product I get it's never enough. Then I've been having this paranoid feeling that someone is watching me."

"Son, you need to hurry up and get out of this lifestyle. Go legit. Invest your money into something long term. I might've started out in the drug game, but I used my head. I own just about all of Harlem. There's not a laundromat, bodega or daycare center that I don't have my money in. There's going to come a time when your gonna want to settle down and have a family of your own. You're not gonna be able to do that selling drugs. If there's not some stickup boy watching your every move then you have to worry about the police. Who wants to be afraid to let their children go outside in fear that someone is going to kidnap them for ransom. In this line of work not only are you in danger but also the people you love."

Every word Jimmy said weighed heavy on Murda's mind. He couldn't disagree with him one bit. Yeah, he was getting money and had a couple of cars, but other than that he had nothing to show for it. Well, he did help Sharnese open her beauty salon, but he put it in her name. He really didn't have much of anything that could help him out If he ever got caught in a jam. First thing in the morning he was going to look for some real estate.

"I feel you on that. I'm about to start doing things a lot differently. The drugs aren't my problem though."

"What is it then?"

"I've got a minor situation with this nigga name Kas."

"Son, look at me," Jimmy grabs his head firmly so that he could understand what he was about to say. For Murda to be his son he sure didn't use good judgment all the time. Murda should have known by now the only way to solve problems was to eliminate them permanently. Out here in these streets, you can't allow beef to carry on. Jimmy wanted Murda to feel every word he was about to say. "Is the nigga still alive and breathing?

"Yeah. Why?" Murda asked confused. His head was starting to pound as the summer heat continued to shine.

"Then IT'S NOT A FUCKING PROBLEM!" Big Jimmy shouted. Hearing his father speak to him that way sent chills up his body. He had never been that hostile to him in his entire life.

"I'm trying, I just can't find the nigga."

"Son, you're really starting to disappoint me. Now normally don't get involved with this street shit, but you're my only son," Big Jimmy hesitated for a few minutes. He wasn't sure as to what he was about to say next. "Once you find out his location we'll both go handle this situation."

"I can't let you do that," Murda couldn't have that on his conscious. If something was to happen to his father he would lose his mind.

"You're not letting me do a damn thing. I'm doing this because you're moving very sloppy. You're so focused on that damn girl, you're not handling business properly," Jimmy had to take a pull from his cigar to calm his nerves. *My son could not have gotten this shit from me. He's worried about some pussy when there's a nigga out here wanting to blow his damn head off. I see now it's time for me to come out of retirement and show these young boys how things are supposed to be done.* "Now get up out of here. You've got some research to do," he said.

"Alright Pops, I'll hit you later."

"Nah Son, don't hit me until it's time to put in work."

After having that conversation with his father Murda need some of that *White Widow* to relax. As soon as he gets into his car, he grabs the Dutch pack from out the glove compartment and sparks his half of blunt. For a minute he thought he was in Amsterdam somewhere. Weed was such a wonderful thing to him. He could care less who didn't agree Weed was not a drug. If anything, it was a healer. Well, it healed all his problems at the current moment.

******

Sharnese sat in the office of her salon going over upcoming appointments. Ever since the grand opening business had been booming. She now had clientele coming from all over the United States to get their hair done. Things were certainly looking good for her. Her mind was no longer on the drama Murda had caused in her life. Yes, she was still heartbroken, but life goes on.

She couldn't lie she missed the hell out of Murda. As much as she wanted to pick up the phone and call him, her pride wouldn't allow her to do it. She had opened to him about her past and he still took her love for granted. She could forgive me for cheating, but a baby was a different story. Hell, she didn't even have any kids. That was a hard pill to swallow. Her phone rings and it takes her mind off Murda.

"Hello?" she said to the strange voice on the other end of the phone. She didn't recognize the number on the Caller I.D.

"Hello, beautiful. I was wondering if you were up for that dinner date you owe me?"

"Hey Kas, how are you?" It finally registers in her head who she's talking to.

"So, are you going to take me up on that dinner date? We don't even have to do dinner we can just go see a movie if you want," Sharnese hesitated for a minute before she finally gives him an answer.

"Why not. I'll meet you at the theater out in Brooklyn."

"No problem, I'll see you at eight. Be easy Ma."

Sharnese hung up the phone grinning from ear to ear. It felt good to get some attention from a man. She had almost forgotten about how good Kas looked the night he gave her a ride home. Just thinking about his tall physique and brown eyes sent a warm sensation between her legs. Times like this she wished she had her vibrator with her. Her thoughts were interrupted by a knock on the door.

"It's open," In walks Murda with a bouquet of roses and a Michael Kors bag. On the inside, Sharnese was jumping up and down. She wanted to kiss him all over his face, instead, she rolled her eyes. "What are you doing here Cortez?" she said calling him by his government name.

"Damn, can I at least get a hey." Sharnese was trying her best to control her emotions, but Murda was making it her for her to do. She hauls off and slaps Murda in his face. *He thinks he can just walk his ass through the door with some gifts and everything is supposed to be cool. Nah, it ain't happening. The same pain I felt his ass is gonna feel too!*

Murda just stood there. He deserved that slap. He had not only broken her heart but all the promises he made her.

"Do you know how embarrassed I felt inside that restaurant? You did the most disrespectful thing you could do. A baby Murda? How could you?" Murda didn't know how to respond. Sharnese didn't deserve any of the pain he had caused her.

"I'm sorry Nese, I know I fucked up with that one. To be honest, I don't even know if that baby is mines."

"Ha-ha," Sharnese laughed out loud. "So, I'm supposed to just be okay with it, and act like nothing ever happened? You know what, leave! Take your gifts and get the fuck out of my office now!" from the look in her eyes, Murda could tell Sharnese wasn't playing with him.

"You know what fuck it. If that's what you want, then you got it. I'm out!"

"Deuces nigga," Sharnese throws up the peace sign and points to the door. For once she had control of something and she wasn't about to let up until she was ready. All her life people had taken advantage of her. No more was she allowing it. Times like this she wished she had a father. Maybe if he was in her life to give her the rundown on men, she wouldn't be so naïve. It seemed like the people she tried to have a relationship with only ended up hurting her. After screaming at Murda she was literally drained of her energy. It was time for her to close the shop and prepare for a night out with Kas.

Murda was furious with the way Sharnese had just carried him. If she wanted to act like she didn't care, then so would he. *You know what fuck her. I chase money, not bitches. The fuck I look like chasing her. From here on out everything is strictly business.* Murda didn't have time for all the extra stuff he had going on. Murda needed to start focusing. He now sees why his father is being hard on him. He had fallen off, business wise.

******

Normally Money would've been the one in charge, but with Destiny being ready to have the baby soon he had fallen back. Murda couldn't do anything but respect his decision. So, with no choice, he made Pop the head nigga in charge. Besides Money, Pop was the only other person he could trust to make sure things were running correctly. Pop answers on the first ring.

"What's good?"

"Inventory check. How's everything looking over there?" Murda asked.

"Like it's time for a vacation," Pop replied.

"Already? Shit, we just came back."

"Yeah man, they are going crazy over this new shit."

"Alright, I'll see you when it's time to roll out."

"You do that," they end the conversation. Murda had already said too much over the phone.

Murda heads to the headquarters to put in another order. All he needed was confirmation then he and Pop would be on their way down South. There still hadn't been any word on Kas. Murda had a hard time trying to find a vacant parking spot. He had an appointment with a realtor and he was running late. He planned on purchasing a few Brownstones if the prices were right.

"Mr. Rodriguez?" The realtor asked trying to confirm whether she had the right person. She was trying her hardest to remain professional, but Murda was making it hard.

"Natalie," she extends her hand for a shake. Murda looked at her as if he's offended. Shaking his head, no, he grabs her hand and kisses it softly.

"Handshakes are for men, and no disrespect but you are definitely not a man," Murda had noticed the way Natalie was checking him out when he first approached her. She blushes in embarrassment.

"Um, let's get inside. It's kind of hot out here," As soft as Murda's lips were on her hand, she could only imagine what he could do with them between her legs.

As if Murda was reading her mind he licked his lips and said, "let's go,"

Jesus this man done licked his lips just like LL Cool J. I'll be on that dick before he leaves here today. Natalie was a pro at seducing men. Anytime a young black man was interested in buying some property she automatically assumed they had money. Brownstones weren't cheap. It's not like Murda wanted to buy one or two, he wanted to buy the entire block. If he was ever to get caught up in a bond, he could rely on the money from his tenants. As they walked into the first set, Natalie made sure she locked the door behind them. She didn't want any interruptions while the two of them were alone.

"In this one here, there are three bedrooms and one and a half baths. As you can see the wall is going to need to be repainted.

Nothing major though. Now if you would look to your right this is the kitchen. All the appliances are brand new. The last owner stayed up to date with taking care of this place. Through the kitchen door is where you'll find the dining room."

Murda was impressed with what he saw. His mind was already made up. He was buying it, no questions asked. His mind was too busy staring at Natalie's ass to pay attention to anything else she was saying. The tightly fitted sundress she had on did very little to hide any of curves. Murda couldn't resist massaging his dick. Natalie saw what Murda was doing from out the corner of her eye. On cue, she dropped her folder and when she bent down to pick them up Murda got a full view of her honey-colored ass. Her thong was caught between her pussy lips.

"Was that a subliminal message? If you want the dick that's all you have to say. Shit, we're both grown."

Natalie's professionalism went out the window. If she had to settle for a sample then she would.

"Well since you put it like that, let's get to fucking," she led him down the hall into one of the bedrooms. There was nothing in the room except for a twin sized bed. Murda was not about to make a fool out of himself by lying on the small bed. It wasn't like he was about to make love. He was simply gonna give her a few pumps, signs the contract and be out. When he looked up Natalie was already on the bed with her ass tooted up in the air. She was ready to go. Murda pulled out a Magnum condom and Natalie frowns her face.

"You don't have to use on those, I'm clean."

"Nah shawty, if we fucking I'm wearing one of these," *This bitch must be crazy if she thinks I'm going up in her raw. I'll be damn if I get caught up in anymore baby mama drama.*

Natalie didn't want to ruin her chance of getting with Murda so she went ahead and cooperated. Murda eased inside her and she let out a slight moan. She didn't expect him to be that big. He grabbed ahold of her thick hips and pounded forcefully.

"Thank you, Jesus!" Natalie hollered out each time Murda worked his way in and out of her tunnel. Matching his rhythm, she begins throwing her hips back. Murda watched her ass bounced back and forth until he shot his load in the rubber. It took Natalie a few minutes to get herself together. She never had a quickie feel that good before. Her clit was still throbbing. If it was up to her Murda would be getting the properties for free. With the way he blessed her with the dick, she had to knock the price down.

"I've seen enough. Where can I sign the contract?" Just that easy, Murda had purchased his first piece of property and it wouldn't be his last. Once he was finished going through all the paperwork Natalie handed over the keys.

"Well, congratulations Mr. Rodriguez. If there's anything else I can do for you please feel free to contact me any time of the day. I'm available twenty-four hours."

"Yeah, I'll do that," Murda knew he wouldn't be calling her for anything else unless it was business related. He was positive this wasn't her first time pulling a move like that. If she'll fuck on the job, then there's no telling how many men had fucked her. She had the nerve to think he was going to hit raw. As bad as AIDS were, she wasn't about to have him walking around looking sick. Murda smiled as he walked to his car. He had listened to his father's advice

******

Sharnese sat in the living room with Mama Peaches watching the evening news. It had been months and they still hadn't heard from Brooklyn. It was starting to take a toll on Mama Peaches. Wrinkles were starting to form in her once smooth face and grey strands were starting to appear in her hair. Every day she worried about Brooklyn's safety. Thankfully her sister down south had volunteered to take custody of the kids until Brooklyn got her life together. Her innocent children didn't need to be involved with what she had going on.

Brooklyn's disappearance wasn't the only thing troubling her mind. Sharnese's mother was scheduled to be released from prison within the next few days. She didn't know how Sharnese would react to the news. It had been years since she'd seen her mother. The last time she tried to visit her, Tonya told her never to come back.

"Sharnese, I have something I need to speak to you about."

"Okay, hit me with it," Sharnese says taking a seat on the couch. Mama Peaches scratched the wig cap sitting on top of her head. She knew this was going to a touchy issue for Sharnese, but she 'd rather tell her now than for it to be a surprise.

"Well…Your mother is getting released this week," Mama Peaches blurts out. Sharnese doesn't know how to respond, let alone feel. The memories she had of her mother were not good ones. Just the thought of everything her mother took her through causes her to cringe. Sharnese wanted more than anything in the world to have a relationship with her mother, but it seemed like the more she tried the more her mother pushed her away. It hurt her to see other females out with their mother's celebrating Mother's Day. She felt like she was finally ready to face the demons that her mother was possessed with. She had questions that she needed answers to. Especially the ones pertaining to her father.

"Good, it's time for us to finally sit down and have a real conversation." Many people would've thought she was crazy for still wanting to deal with Tonya. At the end of the day, Tonya was still her mother and that was something she couldn't change no matter how much she wanted to.

Hearing Sharnese express her feelings about her mother made Mama Peaches want to come clean about her past. Every time Brooklyn or Sharnese would ask her anything she would brush them off. It was time for to reveal her secret life. Everyone has done some things they aren't proud of. Mama Peaches never told anyone she felt like Brooklyn's lifestyle was her fault.

"There's also something else I want to talk to you about."

"Okay, and what is that?" Sharnese asked.

"Well…I know by now you realize that I'm always concerned about your cousin Brooklyn. I feel like I'm to blame for her behavior."

"Now Mama Peaches you know you can't fault yourself for her actions," Sharnese was confused as to where the conversation was headed. She didn't understand her grandmother's reasons, but she knew they had to be good.

"Hush chile and let me finish. Back in my younger days, I had my own escort service. I was what you would call a madam. I provided services to all the high-class people in the major leagues. There wasn't a soul around here who didn't know who Madam Peaches was. You see I started out tricking myself. Working those tracks, I saw all the money the pimps were making so I was like hell, I might as well make some paper too. Each day young runaway girls would appear and instead of giving them good advice

I preyed on them. Most of them were very weak-minded, so it didn't take much convincing. The only thing I saw was money. Greed got the best of me. it didn't matter what they wanted as long as their money was right."

Sharnese was speechless. She surely wasn't expecting Mama Peaches to reveal something like that. It explained why she was always so hard on Brooklyn about changing her ways. *Well, I'll be damn. My grandmother was once a whore turned Madam. There's got to be more to this story. Something isn't adding up.*

"So, what made you give it all up? Was it the money or was it guilt?" Sharnese was laying it on her thick. There was no way she was going to pass up an opportunity to ask Mama Peaches questions about her past. It was something she never talked about.

"Both, the love for money had me doing things I would never do. Where so the guilt ate at me because the girls were so young," During Mama Peaches days as a Madam she had become pregnant with Sharnese's mother Tonya, and Brooklyn's mother Jackie. The two sisters were fraternal twins. They didn't resemble one another at all. Even with her being pregnant she never once saw it as a reason to quit. In return, Jackie ended up strung out on cocaine and pregnant with Brooklyn at just sixteen. Jackie put Brooklyn on to the game at a very young age. While she would be in bed servicing her clients, she would have Brooklyn hide in the closet the entire time and raid their pockets. It was sort of like a family thing.

Sharnese looks at the black square shaped clock on the wall. It was just about time for her to meet Kas at the movies. “Sorry to cut this moment of truth short, but I have somewhere I need to be heading to. We’ll talk more when I get back.”

“Baby, just be careful out there,” Mama Peaches walks Sharnese to the door, watching her as she makes it down the street safely.

Chapter Nineteen

When Brooklyn tried to open her eyes, she couldn't see anything. Everything around her was pitch black. She tried letting out a muffled scream, but it was of no use. There was some kind of rag tied around her mouth. Fidgeting with her fingers, she could feel the rope around her wrists. She had no recollection as to how she had gotten to where she was. The bag over her face made it nearly impossible to catch her breath. Back and forth she rocked in the chair hoping to make some kind of noise. Footsteps could be heard coming down the steps.

"Here you go Unc, she's all yours."

"Good looking nephew. I have something special in store for her."

The two men dap each other up. Brooklyn recognizes the voices as Jean-Claude and Mark. Brooklyn's body shivers in her fear as the footsteps become close to her. Jean-Claude snatches the bag from over her head. A wet sound could be heard hitting the basement's floor. She hadn't seen him since the night she had robbed him.

"Well, well, well, look who we have here," Jean-Claude draws his hand back and smacks her dead in her face. Since she was tied up she had no choice but to take the pain that was being inflicted upon her. Jean-Claude removed the rag from her mouth. Forcefully grabs a handful of her hair and kisses her sloppily in her mouth. It was downright disgusting. Throw-up escapes the corner of her mouth. Particles of food land on her outfit.

"Don't worry I'm not going to kill you…just yet," He said with the most sinister grin on her face. Jean-Claude didn't have plans on killing her at all. Brooklyn was a gold mine. With the exotic look he carried, he knew men back in his native land who would pay top dollars to have her in their brothels. Every dime she had taken from him, he planned on making her work it off. In the corner of the basement was a queen-sized bed with bright camera lights shining over the area. Jean-Claude had ties to the black-market porn industry. One by one different men took turns violating Brooklyn's body. Although she took her clothes off for a living, she had never felt so degraded. She fought back every tear that threatened to escape her eyes. If she wasn't anything else, she was a fighter.

Lord, is this my punishment for my scandalous ways? If I make it out alive, I'm taking my kids and relocating. I want out! After a few hours, Brooklyn became immune to the pain. Her clothes were stained with blood and cum. On the outside, she fought hard to remain strong, but on the inside, she felt like a helpless little girl. Brooklyn breathed a sigh of relief when the last man finished getting his rocks off. Right before putting on his pants, he turned and urinated all over her body. The stench of his piss was so strong, she was bound to throw up again. The cameraman was still in the corner making sure he captured every moment on tape.

"Good job my new money maker," Jean-Claude was having a field day torturing Brooklyn. He wanted to make an example out of her. He was still having a hard time trying to recover from that loss. His connect from the Shower Posse had been harassing him about the missing money. They didn't care about him being robbed. It was either pay what he owed or be slayed. Excuses were for the weak. In actuality, he couldn't blame anybody but himself. He knew better than to have his re-up money around a trick.

The look on Brooklyn's face was one of a mad woman. If looks could kill, he would be sitting in a pit of fire, burning in hell. Jean-Claude saw the evil look on her face but he paid her no mind. The expression he wore made him want to torture her even more. Out of nowhere, an idea popped into his head. Upstairs in the kitchen was a fresh batch of heroin. He didn't have time for her to be rebelling against paying customers. Losing more money would only anger him even more. He disappeared up the stairs and returned minutes later carrying a syringe in one hand and an elastic band in the other. Roughly grabbing her arm, he jabs the needle in her arm. All of a sudden, a warm feeling rushes through her body. Using what little salvia, she has, she tries to wet her mouth. Unable to keep her eyes open, she starts to nod in and out. Brooklyn felt like she was Superwoman. In her eyes, there was nothing she couldn't conquer. The high she was feeling was a powerful one. Her body began to feel sluggish. It wasn't long before sleep became her best friend.

"Aye Unc, let me holler at you for a minute," Mark was trying his best not to let his anger surface. His job was completed. He wanted his money.

"What's up nephew?" There was no one around but them at the time so they felt no need to talk with their Jamaican accents.

"I was wondering when you were going to have that loot for me?" *I don't know why he trying to prolong paying me my fucking money. Shit like this is why I don't look out for people, especially family.*

Jean-Claude already had it set in his mind that he wasn't paying Mark. All the times he looked out for him, Mark should've been doing it as a favor. It was bad enough Brooklyn had been staying with him for the longest before he finally turned her in. If it came down to it, he had no problem getting rid of Mark either. Money was definitely the root of all evil.

"Yeah about that. I've decided I'm not paying you shit!" Mark was certain he had heard him wrong.

"Come again," *My ears must be clogged because I know this nigga just didn't say he wasn't paying me.*

"No, you heard me right the first time. I'm not giving you a fucking dime. It took you forever and a fucking day to deliver her to me. Charge it to the game, and take it as a lesson learned. You always ask for a deposit upfront," Mark ran his hands over his face and through his long dreads. He was pissed his uncle had fucked him over. He had risked his life and freedom transporting a body. Anything could've transpired during that time. Mark's conscience began to eat at him, once he thought about the things he saw happening to Brooklyn. *Here I am abiding by this "family over everything" bullshit and my own blood pull a move on me. I done watched this girl get violated all kinds of ways. What the hell was I thinking? That's somebody's mother and daughter out there. If niggas would have done that to my moms, they wouldn't be alive to tell the next man about it.* Mark knew he had to help Brooklyn get out of there. It was the least he could do.

Brooklyn was stretched out across the grimy sheets, knocked out cold. She was drained physically and mentally. In her dreams she could've sworn she saw the lights taking her to heaven, but she knew that couldn't be true. She had done too much dirt to be walking through anyone's gates to paradise. The effects of the drugs were beginning to wear off. In a blink of an eye, she had sunken into a deep depression. She began to wonder if she was following in the footsteps of her junkie mother.

Like Sharnese, Brooklyn didn't have much of a relationship with her mother either. For as long as she could remember, Jackie was always in and out of rehab. She would stay clean for a while and then turn around and do the same shit. The hate Brooklyn had for her mother was real. Often, she blames her whorish ways on her mother. *Maybe if she didn't stay high all the time, then maybe I wouldn't be like I am today. Maybe if she would've been there when I needed her, then I would know how to do more than just open my legs.* Her mind carried her back to when she was ten years old. The day that changed her life forever.

Sixteen years earlier…

Jackie had just gone done doing the usual, turning tricks. Now that she had her money the only thing on her mind was finding a local drug dealer. She needed her daily fix bad. Brooklyn had been in the closet the entire time watching her mom do it to the older black man. Mr. Tom, he owned the local corner store. Brooklyn hated being alone with me. The vibe she got from him always made him uncomfortable and she had every right to feel that way. Tom had just been released from prison a few months ago for molesting a little girl. He would bribe the neighborhood kids with free candy and chips from his store so that he could have his way with them. He was a sick bastard. He had a wife at home, yet he still chose to mess with underage girls. Tom had seen Brooklyn peeking out the crack in the closet.

"Come on sweetie, you don't have to be afraid," he sat on the edge of the bed naked. Stroking his short, stubby dick back and forth. She looked around hoping her mother would come rescue her from the nightmare she was having. It never happened.

Tom rubbed Brooklyn's premature breasts. He didn't care that she was just a child. The only thing he saw with his eyes was her vagina. Brooklyn jumped back in fear. She knew what Tom was doing wasn't right. Using the sleeve of her shirt, she wiped away her tears. Tom grew impatient. Roughly he threw Brooklyn on the bed. Once on top of her, he forced his manhood inside of her virgin walls. Blood ran down her legs, but he didn't care. Good thing he was only a minute man. He didn't say a word once he was finished. He grabbed his clothes and left the room.

Brooklyn laid there sobbing uncontrollably. She was trying to figure out what she did to deserve the torture. She could barely move her legs as she tried to get off the bed.

"Girl, what are you crying for?" Jackie yelled as she burst through the door.

"Mam that man…he hurt me."

"Child, please. It always hurts the first time," Jackie said nonchalantly.

"You're a woman now and you better remember the power of pussy is serious. You never let a man between your legs without paying. These men got to pay to play. Ain't in this world free."

Brooklyn shook her head at her mother's lesson on men. How could she tell her daughter such a thing at a young age? As much as Brooklyn wanted to hate her mother, something inside her wouldn't allow it. The woman who was supposed to protect her from harm fed her to the wolves. Once the drugs consumed her body Jackie was oblivious to everything except money. Jackie pushed her into the bathroom to clean herself up. In the mirror Brooklyn no longer saw a ten-year-old girl. The reflection that stared back at her she didn't recognize. In her place was a woman who hated men. There was no love in her heart. From that day on she made a vow to use men for their money. If it didn't make dollars, it didn't make sense.

Present day…

Hours later, her high had worn off. She was now drenched in sweat as her body began to suffer from withdrawal. Brooklyn rocked back and forth, holding her stomach as she screamed out in pain. The pain she was feeling was much worse than childbirth. The thought of killing herself crossed her mind. she would have rather been dead than to suffer for another second.

"Somebody help me!" her cries for help went unheard. The only response she heard was laughter. Jean-Clause already had the dope waiting for. This time he didn't bother checking for a vein. He just stuck the needle wherever it would fit. Brooklyn's next scene was scheduled to start in a few minutes.

Two African twin brothers appeared out of nowhere. They had a fetish where they both had to have sex with the same girl at the same time. It was weird. Both brothers shared kids with the same women. The brothers wasted no time taking off their clothes. Brooklyn drifted in and out of reality. She couldn't grasp what was going on. For some reason, her high didn't last as long as it did the first time. One of the brothers had his hands wrapped around her throat. Her air circulation was cut off. She couldn't breathe.

"I can't breathe," Brooklyn struggled to say with what little air she had. The men kept right on pumping furiously. With very little strength she kicks like a deranged animal. Finally, she manages to claw at one of the men's eyes, it only turned him on.

"You like it rough I see." Flipping her over on her side, he shoves his dick inside of her anus. The pain from it sent her body into shock. Mark was disgusted by the site before his eyes. From where he stood he couldn't tell if Brooklyn was dead or alive. Her body laid their motionless. Mark humped back when he felt a tap on his shoulder.

"Yo Unc! You can't be doing shit like that."

"Shut the fuck up! Ya scared ass should've been paying attention."

Why does this nigga keep talking to me like I'm some lame ass, nigga? It's clear Unc doesn't respect his life. If he did he would reconsider the way he talks to me.

"Yo for real chill with the way you're talking to me." Mark was growing tired of his uncle disrespecting him. Family or not, he would end his life. Jean-Claude gets up in Mark's face. Spit flew everywhere. Mark could tell Jean-Claude was amped on drugs. If he had to put his finger on it, he would've guessed it was cocaine. He had tried it a few times himself. Jean-Claude must've been feeling himself. Mark him a couple times and he felt invincible.

"Better yet, get ya dumb ass over here and help me give this bitch her medicine," Mark throws his hands up in the air and protested.

"No! I don't want any parts of this shit. The deal was I deliver her and you pay me my money. Since you didn't keep up with your part of the deal, you're on your own." Jean-Claude was heated. The coke in his system altered his thinking. He pulled out his gun and pointed it at Mark. The red light beamed on his forehead. One wrong move and Mark would be history. It was a good thing Mark kept his gun on him at all times.

"Tick-tock, gunshot!" Jean-Claude taunted as he pulled the trigger. Mark closed his eyes, ready to meet his maker.

Click!

The gun jammed.

Click! Click! Click!

He continued to pull the trigger. It was useless. He threw his hands up surrendering. "Aye nephew, you know I wasn't going to shoot you right?" Jean-Claude laughed trying to play it off. Mark didn't want to hear anything he had to say. The sound of his gun had confirmed his decision. One shot to the head was all it took to end his life. Jean-Claude's body made a thud sound as he hit the pavement. Blood splattered across the walls. Brooklyn heard the gunshots, but she was too sore to move. Mark placed a sheet across her body and she tensed up in fear. She couldn't take any more torture. Her body shook violently as the cold chills overcame her.

"Calm down, I'm not going to hurt you," Mark tried his best to reassure her that he was harmless. If he was her, he wouldn't believe him either. Confusion was written over Brooklyn's face. How could she believe a word he spoke? When this was the same man that had brought her here. She thought about the circumstance and realized she didn't have much of a choice. It was either trust that he would get her to safety, or lay there and die. Giving up was not an option for her. She still had things she wanted to accomplish. Mark knew he didn't have much time left. He had to get them both out of there before someone discovered Jean-Claude's body.

Brooklyn nodded her head in agreement. Her throat itched, and her mouth was dry, but she still managed to get out a few words before passing out again. "Just promise me you'll get me back to Brooklyn," she coughs up little specks of blood.

"Sshh," Mark places his fingers against his lips, signaling her to be quiet. He needed her to save what little energy she had left until she got to a hospital.

How the hell did I get myself into this shit? I was just trying to make a few extra bucks but nah I ended up committing murder. My uncle at that. All he had to do was pay me my money. Now shawty over here all fucked up on that shit. I saw how scared she was when I touched her. Hell, I would be scared to.

Mark picked Brooklyn up and placed her on his shoulder. Once he reached the car, he placed her carefully on the back seat. With his foot on the gas pedal, he was gone in a blink of an eye.

******

Across town, Kas was at Lowe's purchasing a few materials. "Excuse me, Ma'am, can you direct me to the aisle that has the items on this list?" The woman looked at the list and smiled.

"You must be doing some remodeling," If only she knew what he planned on doing.

"Actually, I am, I decided my bathroom needed a makeover. You know after a while you get tired of looking at the same old thing."

"I can relate. Whenever the season changes, I change right along with it. Well, follow me this way. She grabs an empty cart and pushes it down the aisle. The duct tape and rope was located right behind them. They dry cement and paint were located at the back of the store. Kas thanked her for her help and proceeded to collect his items. White paint was something he had to have. He didn't want any signs of blood left anywhere in his house. Finally done looking for everything he needed. He was ready to check out.

"I'm glad you were able to find everything."

"So am I."

"Your total comes to four hundred and seventy-two dollars. Will that be cash or credit?" Kas pulled the hoodie down over his head some more and handed her five one-hundred-dollar bills. He looked out of place with the long sleeve sweatshirt on, considering it was the middle of the summer. He didn't care though. If something backfired, he didn't want the police to be able to identify him on the video camera. Even the pickup truck he was driving had stolen tags on them. He loaded the bags into the truck. There was little time left before his date with Sharnese. He sent her a text making sure they were still on. Once she replied, headed homed to prepare for the night.

"Murda, you done fucked up now son!" Kas shouted out. People passing by assumed he was a little crazy for having a conversation by himself.

******

Sharnese stood in front of the mirror practicing what she was going to say to her mother. It had been years since the two had spoken and she wanted to get everything off her chest. To this very day, she still had nightmares about the beatings her mother would give her. At night she would pray and ask God to remove the ill feelings she had towards Tonya. It was no secret that the women in her family had their own issues. None of the mothers had relationships with their daughters. It was time to end that once and for all. Sharnese hoped the two of them would be able to sit down and have a decent conversation without either of them getting upset.

"Mom, why did you treat me the way you did? What did I ever do to you?" she was so wrapped up in her own world that she didn't realize someone was standing behind her. Hearing the hurt in her daughter's voice brought tears to her eyes. Back then she was such a heavy drinker she would often blackout when she was beating Sharnese. Tonya couldn't blame her daughter for the way she felt. More than anything she was ashamed of her actions. Being a scorned woman caused her to hurt the one person that she loved dearly. During her time in prison, she had begun to see a psychiatrist. Tonya wasn't crazy or anything. She just needed someone to vent to. Someone who understood her pain, and what she had been through.

"I'm sorry Sharnese. From the bottom of my heart, I deeply apologize for all the pain I have caused you," Tonya removed a napkin from her back pocket and dabbed at her eyes. The two women just stared at each other. Sharnese had anticipated this day for a long time, and here she couldn't get a word out. This wasn't the same bitter woman she knew years ago. She wasn't drunk and yelling. There were no insults being thrown her way. Tonya saw that Sharnese didn't have much to say so she continued on with her apology.

"I never meant to hurt you. If anything, I didn't know how to deal with the hurt I was feeling. When you were first born, you looked so much like your father I couldn't stand being around you. Since I couldn't take my frustration out on him, the closest thing next to him was you. If I could take it all back, trust me I would," Tonya knew being mad at Ricky didn't justify how she treated her daughter. She just hoped Sharnese would accept her apology so they could move on and finally have a relationship. Sharnese didn't say a word as she listened to her mother pour her heart out. She was at a point in her life where she just wanted to be at peace with everyone. Sharnese could tell Tonya was being sincere about everything.

"Tonya, I accept your apology but now I want you to see how I felt. For years I struggled with finding myself. Growing up you made me feel like I was nothing. Like there was no purpose for me even being on this earth. My self-esteem was low because of you. I was angry at the world. For a long time, I resented you. Many times, I even contemplated taking my own life. In spite of all that I was able to take all of that negative energy and turn it into something positive. Today I am a licensed beautician and I own a salon. Regardless of everything you said I couldn't do, I still managed to be something."

Sharnese had said more than a mouthful, but she was relieved to have it off her chest. Her mind wandered to Murda and what he could possibly be doing. She missed him dearly. If she could forgive her mother, then it was possible for her to forgive him too. She started to pick up the phone and dial his number but decided against it. She needed a little bit more time alone.

Mama Peaches stood outside the door listening. She was glad to hear that her daughter and grand-daughter were able to put aside their differences. No matter how young she may have dressed and acted, she was getting old. She now only wanted Jackie and Brooklyn to get it together. Jackie was set to get out of rehab in a few months. Completing the program was never her problem, staying clean was. There was something about that fast life that she couldn't stay away from. All it took was for one person to ask where they could find some drugs at, and she would be right back strung out. If it wasn't that then it was the tricking that lured her back in. The greed for money had ruined a lot of lives and corrupted a lot of people.

The saying 'the apple didn't fall too far from the tree' was certainly the case when it came to Jackie and Brooklyn. Mama Peaches just couldn't get her mind off Brooklyn. There was still no word on her whereabouts, and it was driving her insane. Every night she got on her knees and prayed for the lord to send her home. As of now, she hadn't had her prayers answered, but she still had faith. She walked into the family room to Sharnese and Tony engaging in a hug. It brought a smile to her face. It was definitely a Kodak moment.

"I'm glad to see you two are on good term. Please let go of any regrets for tomorrow isn't promised," Mama Peaches said as she ran her fingers through her hair.

"Mama you must think you're still twenty-five years old, with this blonde hair," Tonya knew her mother was a piece of work. She had been locked away for eight years and her mother hadn't changed a bit.

"Chile, please. I'm not twenty-five, but I can still do the same things as these young chicks. You better sit back and take some notes. I might even be able to teach you a thing or two, but I'm a have to charge you."

"Well do I at least get a family discount."

"Bye Felicia! I need all my coins. Shit, these bills don't pay themselves," they all laughed at Mama Peaches and her foolishness. In another life, she would've definitely been a comedian.

"Mama Peaches, what you know about some bye Felecia?"

"Baby, I be all on urbandictionary.com, I got to stay up with you young folks. You won't catch me slipping like that," Sharnese's laughter was interrupted by the vibrating of her phone. Just that quick she had forgotten about everything with Kas. It was well after eight in the evening, and she didn't want to be out too late. She had appointments in the morning and she wasn't about to miss out on any money.

"As much as I hated to leave, I'm afraid I must get going."

"Already?" Tonya whined. "I just got here."

"I'm sorry but this was already planned. I do hope you're here to stay?" Tonya looked at Mama Peaches for approval.

"Don't look at me with those sad puppy dog eyes. You already know my house is your house. Just don't fuck with nothing in my bedroom," Tonya laughed. She knew Mama Peaches was dead serious. She didn't play when it came to her personal belongings.

"I'll see you later then. Be safe out there."

"Thanks, I will," Sharnese said as she walked out the door.

Sharnese was a few minutes late when she finally made it to the movie theater. Luckily, the movie ended up being canceled due to technical difficulties. They ended up grabbing a bite to eat at a nearby Applebee's. They sat in silence as they waited for their food. Kas was growing irritated by the lack of communication. He didn't know why though. It wasn't like he planned on making her his girl or anything.

"Are you always this quiet?" he asked breaking her train of thought. As much as she wanted to engage in the conversation, she couldn't get her mind off Murda. She had forgiven her mother, but she was still having a hard time getting past Murda's deception. She quickly conjured up a story in her head to tell him.

"I'm always like this around people I don't really know, why?" She was hoping he brought the lie she had just told him. One thing she hated was a persistent nigga. That was a big turn-off in her book. She couldn't lie. He was definitely a site to see, but he still didn't compare to Murda. Kas ran his hands over his head. His waves flowed so evenly if you looked too fast you were sure to get seasick.

"I can dig it. So, you got to school or something?" Kas was trying his best to make small talk. He could tell something was on her mind. *This bitch probably over there thinking about that nigga Murda.* Kas had to tame his thoughts. It didn't take much to get him off. A lot of people knew him as Kas, but the ones who knew him personally he was Crazy Kas. He didn't acquire the name because it sounded good.

"I just graduated from cosmetology school. I own a salon," talking about her accomplishments made her feel good about herself. It had even taken her mind off Murda for the time being.

Another basic bitch. Just about every girl in the hood does hair for a living. Why can't these broads be more original? If they not doing hair, then they're either selling clothes or in the nursing field. Kas shook his head. He acted as if he was interested as he listened to Sharnese go on about the different clients she had. The waitress placed their food on the table. It took so long for her to bring it, he lost his appetite. Sharnese devoured her boneless buffalo wings with ranch dressing. She started to order a drink but decided against it. She didn't know that much about Kas to be drinking around him.

"Is there anything else I can get you?" The waitress politely asked. She was just doing her job, praying that Kas left a decent size tip. From the clothing he had on, he looked like he could spare a couple dollars.

"Yeah, let me get a container for my food," he hadn't touched a thing on his plate. "You need anything before we leave?"

"No thank you, I'm good," Sharnese said still stuffing wings into her mouth.

"That'll be it."

"Alright, I'll be right back with your change and receipt," he hands her a hundred-dollar bill and tells her to keep the change. Kas couldn't help but stare as she walked away.

"Damn, if you're going to stare that hard you might as well ask for her number," Sharnese didn't care about him looking. He wasn't her man. It was simply a respect thing. She was sure he was going to whip his dick out and start jerking off at the table.

"My bad, I'm an ass man, that's all," while they were in the restaurant Kas had Jermaine pick his car up. He needed to have an excuse for Sharnese to go to his house. It was time to get down to business. He was tired of playing around.

"If you don't mind can you give me a ride to my crib? My homeboy car broke down so I told him to come get mines," Kas was hoping she didn't say no.

"It shouldn't be a problem," Kas put his address inside her GPS. It was like a forty-five-minute drive from their location. With the way, Sharnese was driving they would be there in no time.

Chapter Twenty

Fetty Wap's *Trap Queen* played from the speakers of Murda's red A8 Audi. He was on his way to collect some money. It was Friday night and he didn't want any mishaps his money. His phone buzzed in the cupholder, he looked at the screen and hit ignore. It was nobody but Natalie calling. She had become a pest ever since he dicked her down. *Give a bitch some good pipe and they lose all their common sense.* Murda could've answered the phone, but he didn't feel like listening to her whine about being used. Pulling into the yard of one of his trap houses, he gets out the car and daps everyone up. Normally he would've fussed about people hanging out in front of the house. The last thing he needed was for the police to be on his back. When he walked in Pop already had everything waiting for him. The money was placed neatly inside a black duffel bag. Business was booming. The numbers spoke for itself.

"Everything good?" Murda asked making sure everything was well stocked. It was the weekend so he had to do an inventory check. There was no way he was going to miss out on the guaranteed money. Especially since he knew all the partying took place Friday through Saturday.

"Yea Fam, we good. Now get on out of here. I got this," Murda loved how the young boy took control. When Murda promoted him, he took the job to his heart, and so far, he hadn't fucked up yet. With the duffel bag in hand, Murda exited the house as quickly as he came.

*****

Sharnese was at Kas house in no time. The area he lived in was nice and quiet. There weren't many other houses around. If you wanted to commit a crime, it would be the ideal place. Sharnese was impressed when she walked into the living room. For Kas not to have a girlfriend he had good taste in decorating. The cream and navy-blue décor blended well together. She just knew he had to have a girlfriend or female he was messing around with.

"You sure you don't have a girl?" she asked. She didn't believe he decorated the house himself. Hell, most men couldn't match colors together properly.

"I'm positive, it's just me. I let my mom do all the decorating and shit. I just picked out the colors and paid for everything."

Kas was an only child and a mama's boy at that. Everything he did, he included his mother. He admired how strong she was. It wasn't easy being a single mother, and raising a boy with no help. He didn't know anything about his father. His mother often switched her story up whenever he asked about him. first, he was his father was killed in a drug deal gone bad. Then there was the time she told him he was in prison. He didn't know what to believe, so eventually, he stopped asking. He figured there had to be some bad blood between the two. She would often blame his way of living on not having a father figure and she was right. With Kas not having a male to guide him through life, the streets ended up raising him. His teenage years were the worst. He never graduated from school, due to always getting suspended. Going to school was the last thing on his mind. The only time he went was to bust a lick. If it wasn't making him money then he didn't have time for it.

"That explains a lot. Can I use your bathroom?

"Yeah, it's down the hall to the left," The sound of the door closing made Kas realized what he'd just done. *Man, what the fuck was I thinking? I hope she doesn't see the shit in the bathtub.*

Sharnese was in the bathroom signifying. She wasn't convinced that he lived in the house alone. It was too spacious for one person. She opened the medicine cabinet and there was nothing in there except a small bottle of Scope mouthwash and some Colgate toothpaste. *Maybe he was telling the truth, after all.* There were no feminine products in the cabinets at all. As a last resort, she pulls back the shower curtain hoping to see some type of female body wash.

Her mouth dropped open. There were two wooden handmade chairs that resembled the ones used for execution. Her body quivered in terror when she saw her and Murda's name written in red paint. She doesn't know what the hell was going on. She just knew she needed to get out of there. Her only way to escape would be jumping out of the window. There was only one problem. She was on the second floor. Trying to be quiet as possible, she turns the trashcan upside down and places it beside the toilet. Using them both as a boost she's able to reach the window. "Fuck!" she hollers out loud. The windows on had padlocks on them. Unless she had a key, she wasn't getting out that way.

Kas marched down the hallway. Sharnese had been in the bathroom too long. He figured she'd seen the chairs by now. *Why couldn't she just piss and get the hell out? But nah this bitch had to go snooping around.* It was time for him to speed up the process. *Boom* The sound of the door being kicked in catches Sharnese off guard. He cocks his pistol grip. "Going somewhere?" he asks with a sinister look on his face. Sharnese stood there completely baffled. This wasn't the same man, she'd known just moments ago. The sweet gentleman that opened doors had transformed into a deranged lunatic. His eyes were cold as ice.

"What do you want with me?" she demanded to know. She couldn't figure out how she had been caught in the middle of their beef.

"I don't want a damn thing from you. It's Murda I'm after. You just happen to be my way of bringing him here," Sharnese felt like a fool. Then it dawned on her, he must've been watching her the entire time. How else would he have known what she looked like, and the places they go?

"So, you set the whole thing at the restaurant up?" Sharnese asked.

"Something like that. Chanel is a local thot who loves to run her mouth. I overheard her conversation about a nigga named Murda who had plenty of money. I put two and two together and paid her a little piece of change to cause a scene. At the time I knew nothing about her being pregnant with his baby," Kas explained.

Sharnese was furious. Her chest heaved in and out. If he wanted Murda he would have to go through her first. She had made a vow to ride with him till the wheels fell off. All the anger she felt towards Murda was gone. If she got out of this predicament, they were going to fix their relationship. If the baby is his, she was going to make the best out of the situation. It was all or nothing. Sharnese threw a few punches catching Kas in the face. Although she had a small frame, her hands were nothing to be played with.

The punches didn't faze me much. *Whap!* The slap Kas produced was so hard Sharnese felt her lip slit. The taste of her own blood rested on her lips. She opened her mouth to speak but was stopped. *Whap!* The force of the second slap caused her to lose her balance. Somehow, she had tripped over a rug and hit her head against the edge of the bathroom sink. She was out cold.

*****

Murda was downtown at a local pool hall having a few drinks and playing catchup with Money. It had been a while since the pair had last seen each other. Murda took a hit of the blunt and passed it to Money.

"Here man, you look like you need it more than I do," he was right. Money had a lot on his plate. Destiny was due to have the baby anytime now and Mama Peaches had been calling every day asking if he'd seen or heard anything from Brooklyn. As much as he hated his son's mother, he was still worried. Brooklyn had pulled a disappearing act before, but not this long. He'd been to her house several times. The grass was untamed and the mailbox was full. He was certain that he'd seen what looked like dried up blood on the door, but he could've been wrong.

"Talk to me fam what's going on?" Murda had never seen his boy so stressed out. Money was usually the one listening to his problems.

"Man, shit is all fucked up. Ever since Destiny and my baby mama had that fight at the club, she's been missing," Money downed a shot of Hennessey.

"Nah bro, you don't think Des had something to do with that do you?" he asked jokingly. Murda knew what Destiny was capable of if provoked. He didn't know Brooklyn personally, but he had heard many stories of how she got down.

"I don't know. I just find it's kind of strange that's all."

The combination of the weed and alcohol had all types of scenarios running through Money's head. He wanted to question Destiny so bad but didn't want to risk her upsetting the baby. Murda was just about to respond when the ringing of his phone indicated he had a message. The name *Babe* popped across the screen.

"I knew my baby would come back around," he said out loud. When he opened the message, a pain shot through his chest. A bruised Sharnese was slouched over with her wrists clamped down on the chair.

"Hurry, Murda help me!" *This has got to be a sick joke. When I find out who did this their ass is good as dead.* Murda got his answer when Kas appeared in front of the camera.

Kas rhymed his favorite saying "Murda, Murda, Murda, I'm a murder Murda," he laughed like it was the funniest thing in the world. "It's now seven o'clock on the dot. You got exactly two hours to get here before I decide to blow ya bitch head off," Kas places the camera back on Sharnese. "Are there any last words you'd like to say right now?"

"Fuck you!" Sharnese says as she spits in his face. Kas wiped the spit from his face. He was about sick of Sharnese. She was a feisty bitch. He wasn't sure if he'd be able to keep her alive much longer. Without hesitation, he slammed the butt of the gun in her face. That was the last Murda saw of Sharnese before the video cut off. Another message came through with the address. Money didn't need an explanation as to why Murda had stormed off. He had heard the entire thing. If it was Destiny, he would've done that same thing.

Murda didn't give his dad a warning call. He just popped up announced driving up the lane like a maniac. Carmen and Jimmy came running out the house. They thought something was on fire until they realized it was the smell of rubber burning. The smoke from the tires said enough. Murda was heated about something.

"Carmen go inside the house while I have a talk with our son," Carmen did as she was told.

"Son, calm down and talk to me. What's the problem?"

"I need all the guns and ammunition you got. It's time to go to war! That nigga got Sharnese." Murda chokes up and tears fell from his eyes as the image of her bruised faced played in his head.

"Say no more," they both walked into the house where a black bag was waiting for them. The bag contained all types of artillery.

Murda decided on two .45's. Big Jimmy was old school, he grabbed a couple revolvers. He couldn't risk the other guns jamming on him. Jimmy's Yukon, Denali awaited them out front. He wasn't too trusting of Murda's car at the moment. He could still see a bit of smoke rising from the tires. Running out of weapons was the least of Jimmy's worries. He kept a few guns hidden in all his vehicles. Murda gave Jimmy the address and they were on their way.

*****

Big Jimmy looked around and examined the neighborhood. They were amongst the upper-class white folks so they had to be extremely careful. Murda's heart was beating faster than normal. It might've been the rush he was feeling. He was amped up and ready for war. Jimmy and Murda walked around to the back door. Murda twists the knob and it's unlocked. Cautiously, they enter through the kitchen unsure if Kas was alone. Murda spots Sharnese in the living room and he runs to her rescue. Her breathing was very shallow and she had a busted lip. Murda wanted to kill everything moving. He couldn't fault anybody but himself. Sharnese was too good of a person to be involved with his drama. Murda cups her head in his hands.

"Sharnese baby, can you hear me?" she nods her head slightly. The blow she encountered earlier still had her in a daze. One minute she was up and alert, the next she was zoning in and out.

"Well, well, well, if it isn't the man of the hour. So nice of you to finally join us," Kas clapped his hands together repeatedly. He always enjoyed taunting his victims.

Big Jimmy stood in the corner unnoticed observing the entire scene. The resemblance between the two men was undeniable. *No, it can't be possible,* he thought. Jimmy looked Kas over once again. His suspicious where confirmed when his eyes rested on Kas neck. In big cursive print, the letters on his neck spelled out the name Diana.

Murda wasted no time pulling out his gun. The safety was already off. All he had to do was pull the trigger and Kas would no longer exist. Murda just knew he had the upper hand until he saw Kas had his gun pointed at Sharnese. Jimmy walks into the room, hoping to defuse the situation.

"Both of you put your guns down," he commanded. Murda and Kas looked at Jimmy and laughed. They both had been dreaming about this day.

"Who the hell are you?" Kas fired a shot at Big Jimmy. The bullet barely misses his face, as it makes a huge hole in the wall. A couple of paintings come crashing down on the floor. Jimmy wasn't sure if he wanted to reveal the information now or wait until he found out for sure.

"Is your mother's name Diana Richards?" he asked. Kas had an angry look on his face. Big Jimmy didn't have much time to come up with some answers. "Yeah that's her and what the fuck does she have to do with anything?"

Pow! Pow! Pow!

Kas was done fucking around. He fired three shots. One of the bullets hit Murda in his right shoulder while the other one barely missed his heart by an inch. Murda's body hit the hardwood floor and a pool of blood starts to form underneath him. He was losing a lot of blood quick. Jimmy hid behind the couch. He was trying to avoid getting shot at all costs, but if he had to shoot Kas to save his own life then he had no problem doing so.

"Son, I'm your father," Jimmy said as he let out a deep breath. Kas was caught off guard. It was a huge pill for him to swallow.

"Then that means he's my… brother," Kas said looking at Murda lying on the floor. During that time Sharnese had regained consciousness, she was able to slip her small hands through the clamps on the chair. Finally, free, she grabs Murda's gun from off the floor. *Pop! Pop! Pop!*

Was all she remembered hearing before she blacked out again.

To Be Continued…

[illegible] come up with some answers" [illegible] said when [illegible] doesn't have to do with anything?"

Now [illegible]

Kas [illegible] one of the bullets [illegible] [illegible] [illegible] [illegible] trying to [illegible] [illegible] he had no problem doing so.

[illegible] Jimmy said as [illegible] [illegible] Kas was [illegible]

[illegible] Kas said [illegible] [illegible] [illegible] [illegible]

[illegible] was [illegible] gone.

To Be Continued

CPSIA information can be obtained
at www.ICGtesting.com
Printed in the USA
LVOW13s2315040618
579618LV00010B/191/P